I0624023

My Novel Year
Savannah Hendricks

Grand Bayou Press

First published by Grand Bayou Press

Library of Congress Control Number: 2025921256

ISBN Paperback: 979-8-9875431-4-6

eBook ASIN : B0FZM8ZM4S

For Film and TV Rights – GrandBayouPress@protonmail.com

Cover design by Savannah Hendricks

Editing: Krista Dapkey

Proofing: Greg Filzen

Annually, 10% of the proceeds from the sale of this book, and all Savannah's books are donated to dog rescue organizations.

READING IS BETTER WITH A DOG - Savannah

Contents

Dedication: For all the authors who dreamed and all the readers who read those dreams.

Special guest appearances by Ox Swanson and his therapy
English Labrador, Bayou, from
Grounded in January & ***Grounded in July***

Chapter 1

Fall

"I can't believe you're doing something so . . . ." My best friend, Amy Strauss, crossed her arms. "So . . . precarious."

My eyebrows lowered in the center as I peered at her on the couch. "I believe the word you're looking for is *amazing*. My life's dream!" I could feel the joy spread through my entire body.

"I was thinking more along the lines of *impossible*."

"It's not a mission, and I'm not Tom Cruise. It's very possible. The opposite of impossible. I'm going to write a novel, not build an entertainment center from IKEA." I wrapped my arms around myself in a hug. The hug I was expecting from Amy when I'd told her the news several months ago that never came. Like when we were teenagers and super eager for the upcoming release of our favorite band's CD at Sam Goody. Instead, Amy just sat there on the corner of my couch, holding the sweating beer bottle, bouncing her right leg as she sat cross-legged.

"What happened to starting small? Take a writing class. Read a book, perhaps from this century."

I waved my hand at her, swiped my wineglass off the counter, and approached the side of the couch. "We both know classic literature is the best. Besides, if I read new releases, then I might lose the spark of creativity muffled by modern novels. You remember when I read the latest Hannah Xander novel set in England during the thirteenth century? I dreamed our manager was a knight jousting against me, and I was trying to break his lance so he'd fall off his horse into a pile of horse poop. Fun times."

Amy nodded her head and kept the opening of the beer bottle pressed against her lips. "I wish you had. Why do we have the midnight-to-eight-a.m. shift after all our years of service? We're too old to work for an open-twenty-ty-four-hours grocery store."

"We're not old. We just aren't young." I extended my glass of wine in front of me as though I was trying to climb into a dinghy as I sank onto the couch. While I might be thirty-nine, I knew the big four-o was coming a lot quicker than I wanted. Thankfully, Amy had already arrived there a few months ago, and she seemed to be managing just fine. "But that's exactly why I put in for my sabbatical. The rude customers, the leg and back pain from standing in one spot for eight hours. If I didn't do it now"—I waved my hand in the air—"I'll never have time to chase my dream. And I don't want to wait until I retire."

"Hey, we get a thirty-minute lunch." Amy frowned. "I get it, I really do, but still."

I smiled. "It's time to do something for me, myself, *moi*. Get away from my life here, from the ex-husband's drive-bys, so I can really explore the story, do the research, and write with no distractions."

"I can't believe he's still hanging on to you," Amy said. "But I can get behind the change in scenery, and experiencing the four seasons."

"And half the fun will be going old school, very Jessica Fletcher. Just my thoughts spilling out onto the pages as I *tap-clack* type away on my typewriter. Followed by long days of research at the library with my thermos of hot tea."

Amy choked on her beer and coughed. "Why would you do that?"

"Because I like tea." I sat upright on the couch.

"No, the typewriter. You can't submit the story on typewriter paper. You have to email it."

"I know that. I've been following some of the big-name authors on social media and they talk about distractions being an enormous factor in getting their work done by the deadline. So, moving to a town where I don't know a single person, where I don't have my ex-husband around every corner, and where I don't have access to the internet as I write is exactly what I need."

"Shouldn't you be renting a cabin in the middle of the woods? You know *Misery* it up?"

I sighed and sipped the finest Malbec my grocery store carried—under seven bucks. "I don't plan on kidnapping anyone. The deal for the furnished rental condo *on* the water was a sign. It just fell into my lap. The owner is doing something with Doctors Without Borders or a border without a doctor or a doctor needing a border. Plus, she said the town is quaint in the fall and winter is just the locals, so I can really get a good start on the manuscript before the spring and summer tourists show up."

"Where is this place again?"

"Ocean Cove, in Washington."

"You'll need a jacket and several raincoats." Amy reached her hand toward my knee and gave it a squeeze. "I'm happy for you, but I worry. You're going to be alone, several states away. And they probably have bears."

"On the beach?"

"I don't know. We've lived in Nevada our entire lives; I don't know what lurks around the bushes there. I know this has been your dream since you were in your late twenties. But I don't know." She switched hands with her beer. "I guess I just don't know what I'll do without you at work for an entire year."

"You can come and visit. Besides, a year will fly by, and when I return, I'll hopefully have a manuscript that agents and publishers will fight over." I placed my hand over hers. "I worked so hard to save up enough money to do this, and sacrificed years of vacation time."

"I know, I know."

"I need your support. With my parents gone, and the ex thinking I'm crazy, you're the only one to wish me well."

"Don't make me cry." Amy crawled forward and wrapped her arm around my shoulder. "I love you. And when you leave, I'm left with two kids and a husband. Who will save me?" She laughed and leaned back.

"You poor thing. A great family. Whatever will you do?" I exaggerated a pouty face.

"So, you're really doing this?"

"The temporary renter moves into my townhome next week." I looked around at my boxes of personal items that were headed to storage for a year. "Even though I'm scared, I'm doing it."

Amy rested her hand on the top of the couch. "I would be too. You're incredibly bold to put your life on hold to chase a dream. I could never do that. I mean, I didn't aspire to be a grocery store checker. I just wish I had a dream as big as yours."

"You do. You have dreams for your girls. You have dreams for you and Rob. Travel dreams, kids getting married, grandkids." I choked on the lump that formed in my throat. "Some dreams that I can never have. When I got divorced, I couldn't afford to start over, to start fresh and leave it all behind. I couldn't even get a new set of sheets. This is the freedom I need."

As a teenager, I assumed that I'd know what motherhood was all about one day. My mom sure used it against me a lot, always reminding me, Analena, you'll understand one day when you're a mother. And I kept that statement in my heart until the doctor informed me that motherhood doesn't have to be bound by blood.

"I understand." Amy picked at the label on her beer. "Why can't you just write on your days off?"

"Because while I believe I can write a novel in bits and pieces over the weekends, I also believe that it'll be better to tackle it all at once. And it's not how the big names do it. And I want a chance to be a big name." I looked at Amy and could see she was happy for me, but worry was laced in between. "Please understand and wish me luck."

"I wish you all the luck in the world."

Chapter 2

I was three seconds from reaching the couch and hitting play on a thriller movie when there was a knock at my door. I pondered if I should answer it as I set my heaping serving-for-three—and I'm eating it all—bowl of mac and cheese on the coffee table next to my wineglass.

I peeked through the tiny peephole that was a foot too high for me. On my tippy toes, I recognized the figure outside. When I lowered back down to the soles of my feet, I clenched my fists, grumbling a growl.

Sliding the chain off the door, I pulled it open but blocked the gap. "Dawson."

My ex-husband. No, *the* ex-husband, according to the divorce book I read. If I put *the* in front of *ex* instead of *my* it disconnects me from him, which is important for us both.

Dawson clapped his hands together. "Analena, thank goodness, you've not left yet." He stepped forward, allowing his flip-flops to cover the *e* and *m* on my welcome mat. "Hey, your hair looks nice. I like the reddish color you've got going on there. Is it longer too?"

I flung my hand out like a school crossing guard. "Where are you going? Because you're *not* coming inside."

He frowned. "Why not? I just want to chat. See if I'm too late to change your mind."

"You're about three years too late."

Dawson's neck became one with his chin. *Great, he's trying to figure out math.*

"Three years, when I informed you that you had one year to stop being a jerk. Then I asked for a divorce, which you dragged out for a year. And thus, here we are at one year of legally being divorced." I'm still blocking the path inside.

"Hear me out. I'll go with you. Just the two of us. You can still write, and I'll do whatever it is that people do in Ocean Cave." His eyes narrowed. "Ocean Wave?"

"Ocean Cove."

He clapped and pointed both hands like guns so close to my face that I leaned back. "No. You're staying here. I'm going. And how did you know where I was moving to? I never told you."

"I have my sources." Dawson winked.

"Well, un-source your sources. One of the reasons I'm going is to start fresh."

He shoved his hand in his shorts pocket. "Why not give us another shot. Maybe what we need is time away from here, together."

"Yes."

His face lights up.

"Yes, I need time away from here. No, *we* don't." I pressed my lips together with a half-pity smile. "Dawson, please understand and respect that we're divorced. Nothing is going to change that. This is not some sappy romantic movie where we find our way back to each other and ignore all the reasons our marriage didn't work in the first place."

"Fine. But don't say I didn't put up a fight for us."

I clenched my teeth to prevent myself from responding about how untrue that was on many levels.

"Now, can I borrow your Crockpot?" He crossed his arms.

"It's packed up."

"Then can I have the keys to the storage unit that you put everything in?"

"No, we divided everything, and I got the Crockpot. You never liked anything I made in it anyway."

"That's why I need it. *I'm* cooking."

I gasped, stepped back, and slammed the door.

"So, is that a firm no?" Dawson yelled through the closed door.

I shook my head and returned to the living room, where my mac and cheese was getting cold. Pouring more wine from the pinot bottle sitting on the coffee table, I scooped up the bowl and rested it on the pillow on my lap. But before I hit play, I noticed the absence of silence. A neighbor's dog was barking against the *boom-boom* of a car stereo going by on the street. Off in the kitchen, my refrigerator hummed. And then there was the sound of my heartbeat still thumping loudly in my chest. I picked up my cell phone from the armrest of the couch and opened my notes with my novel year list.

1. Write a best-selling novel

2. Lose thirty pounds

3. Find the happiness I once had

A tear formed as I thought about what Amy said. *Impossible.* Maybe she was right. Maybe all three will end in complete failures. My failed marriage, my struggle with weight, and my job are all reminders of what I don't love about my current life. I took a bite of my now cool mac and cheese, but I was so down in the dumps, I didn't care that at this point the cheese had become a gluey industrial paste. At least the noodles didn't fall off my fork.

My marriage should have worked out, but sometimes those things just don't live up to what we hope. My position as a grocery store cashier was supposed to be temporary until Dawson got his company off the ground, but it never left the hangar. While my townhome is nice, it's not the cute little cottage I always wanted. I dreamed of mini roses in terra-cotta pots on the back patio, a small grassy yard with hummingbird feeders and wildflowers, along with a quaint office where I could type away story after story looking out onto the happenings of my neighborhood. My townhome is on a busy street that never seems to rest, and my backyard is a king-size bed concrete slab. And my weight, the never-ending struggle to feel better about myself when I stood naked in front of the mirror. *Maybe I should get rid of my mirrors.*

However, one goal, my lifelong dream, finally came together better than expected. After years and years of saving and planning, I stumbled upon the most perfectly priced, and hopefully an amazing condo, in Washington. I felt like a kid on Christmas morning when Santa got all the presents right. Regardless, I was scared to take the leap, to leave what I knew, even if what I had was not getting me anywhere I aspired to be.

I tucked my legs under me and continued to eat the cold mac and cheese as I hit play on the remote. Yet, as the movie played, my thoughts drifted more to my life's disappointments than to the characters on the screen. The drive to Washington worried me the most because I could always turn around. And I feared my anxiety would get the best of me and I'd do just that. The only person holding me to my dream was me. Dawson had never supported it back when I first mentioned it. My parents were long gone to guide me in the decision. And while my best friend supported me, Amy didn't want me to leave. She'd attempted to perfect the mental jujitsu she outwardly portrayed while I picked up on the thinly veiled reasons to stay.

When I zoned back into the movie, I realized the main character was an author taking a vacation to write her latest children's book.

"It must be doable if they make numerous movies with this trope."

With each passing minute of the movie, the courage grew stronger inside my heart. And when I crawled into bed that night, I felt like a child before a big adventure. I folded my hands on top of my sheet and stared at the water stains on the ceiling. I really need to get those re-painted. It'd been five months since the roof leaked during a summer monsoon that rolled through Henderson and a palm tree slammed hard enough into the tiles to break a few. It was all sealed up now, but the inside damage was on the back burner when I worked overtime to help cushion my savings and to cover the damage my insurance didn't.

Thump, thump, thump.

My neighbors were having a late-night party, so I rolled over and covered my ears with a pillow. "I won't miss this." But I knew it was going to take a while for me to drift off to sleep, even without the beat of the music.

Chapter 3

"What do you mean you're not out of Nevada yet?" Amy said through my cell phone's speaker.

"I sort of had to make an unexpected stop, technically two. Do you realize how tall Nevada is?"

"Please tell me this doesn't involve Dawson."

"Okay."

The car tires hummed on the highway.

"Analena!"

I clenched the steering wheel as the car swerved, and I righted it. "My stuff is just sitting in storage. He wanted the Crockpot. I told him it was on loan until I get back."

"This is why he thinks there's still hope for you two. You need to stop connecting with him. You shouldn't answer the door when he comes over. Don't answer his texts, his calls," Amy said.

"We can still be friends. Besides, it's not a problem anymore."

"No, you can't still be friends, even in Washington. You got divorced for a reason. Don't return to that unhappiness and the heartbreak."

"It's not like he cheated on me."

"Correct, but a marriage doesn't need infidelity to cause heartbreak."

I nodded my head and sighed. "All of that is behind me now." I glanced in the rearview mirror. "Literally."

"I'll let you focus on driving. Call me when you get there."

"I will, probably pretty late. I won't even make it out of Nevada today. I'm staying in Reno."

"Watch out for the sheriff's department."

"How funny would that be if *Reno 911* were real?"

"Terrifying. Very terrifying."

"But hilarious. Anyways, it's a ten-hour drive to Ocean Cove from Reno, and I'll be getting up *early* to head out. Just after sunrise. My night vision is getting worse. I wish my parents were still around so I could have a heads-up about stuff I didn't expect to experience at our age. Such as having to remove my glasses to read my cell phone, then slide them back on to see the TV."

"Just drive safely on that long, lonely stretch of nothing."

"It's not lonely when I've got music to keep me company."

We said our goodbyes, and I turned up the music as Papa Roach bumped through the speakers. I made my way past a semitruck on my right and gripped the wheel until the wake of the enormous truck passed.

I tapped the steering wheel, switching my thoughts to Ocean Cove and the dreams that lay in front of me. A new town, a new climate, and an entire year of doing what I've always dreamed of. I was getting an opportunity that many didn't, a chance to write a novel uninterrupted. What a joy to be able to focus on being an author and find out what that really meant.

"Hi, I'm Analena," I said aloud, practicing. "Oh, what do I do? Well, I'm an author." I smiled. "Yes, I spend my days creating best-selling novels while I sip on coffee and munch on snacks. No, I don't get out of my pajamas, so sorry to hear you need to dress up for your job."

Not wanting to chance the unknown selection of writing products in Ocean Cove, I packed a replacement ribbon for my typewriter and ten reams of paper. I had notebooks and pens to help me with edits and revisions, along with nonfiction books about plot, self-editing, and story structure for added help. The entire year, from fall to fall, give or take two weeks, I was going to live and breathe everything writing. And I was sure that was how it was done. I'd studied thoroughly via the internet that every author has a process, but they were mostly all the same. I had a well-polished outline, and that was all I needed to dive in.

I had a strict guideline set up along with an even stricter budget to make sure I maintained my savings and didn't run out. Everything from groceries to electricity bills to gas for the car was rationed out over twelve months. The only thing I didn't budget for was health care. But sitting at a desk and lounging in your pajamas all day hopefully meant no chance for injuries or medical crises. Next fall, with any luck, when I returned home to Henderson with a sold manuscript, I could get my annual checkups and return to work before completely running out of savings.

While my dream was to land an agent, I was open to signing with a small publisher. Yet deep down inside, I was hoping to make it as a New York Times Bestseller, and I knew I needed an agent who could make that happen. My dream tree had an extended olive branch of returning to work for a few months and then quitting once I got a contract. Miracles do happen. Although I'd researched the process of self-publishing, to make it as good if not better than traditionally published authors would require too much money, experience, and clout that I didn't have yet. Plus, if I was the next Riley Sager or Dean Koontz, I could make a handsome living from my books. Back in reality land, I knew the chance of that dream coming true was roughly the same as wishing I was as famous as Kate Winslet.

The highway was bedraggled on both sides for miles with long strips of dead grass and muted tones of scrub brushes. With each passing desert shrub, I thought about the outline of my manuscript. The storyline and arc felt strong and held the creative embodiment of what I hoped was a perfect story.

My cell phone vibrated in the cup holder next to my water bottle, and I hit the green button, then speakerphone.

"Hello?"

"We're calling about your car's insurance," a voice recording said.

"Oh, for goodness's sake!" I punched End with my pointer finger so hard I might have sprained it.

Ahead, I noticed a sign for Carl's Jr. and decided my diet could wait until I crossed over the Washington state line. Stretching my legs was a must. Getting up and walking around should lessen the numbness engulfing my rear end and give me a few steps for the day. I could hear my mom's voice in the back of my mind from childhood. *Kick those heels to your bottom, Analena,* she'd say. *Move your legs. If you gain any more weight, the carnies will be trundling your bottom from town to town by low loader.*

The embarrassment of my mom was not just reserved for home but also road trips. It constantly looked like Mom was about to film an exercise video right there at the I-5 rest stop. And Dad with his bulky camera, waving

Mom and I left or right so we could stand perfectly centered at the scenic outlook point. I couldn't imagine what she would think of me today, talk about heavy.

Instead of hitting the Carl's Jr. drive-thru, I parked my faded and dented ten-year-old blue Corolla and got out. My entire trunk was crammed with paper, books, and my typewriter. The back seat was stacked high with clothes, sheets, towels, a few personal items, and toiletries I couldn't live without for the next year. Boxes added bulk, so everything but one box, which occupied the passenger seat, was simply stacked like a game of Jenga across the back seat. It felt as though I was being shipped off to another planet that was void of Walmart and Costco. *Mmm, Costco pizza.*

I climbed out of the car as though I had a broken back and slowly stretched. Even though I was still in the desert, the breeze had a chill to it, and I wrapped my hands around my arms and hurried toward the door. The smell of breaded chicken mixed with grease filled my nose as I entered the vacant dining area.

After ordering, I took my receipt along with my strawberry lemonade in a cup bigger than my head and stood gazing out the large windows to the drive-thru line. My butt tingled as the blood flow slowly eased back into it. A small part of me felt like I needed to do a few hamstring curls. I guess even in death my mother was never really gone from my life.

With my warmish cheeseburger and steaming fries, I headed to a booth in the corner, thinking my bottom would favor the vinyl over my car seat. I did my best to savor every bite, even though there was a sense of shame. Shame from knowing I shouldn't be eating fast food, yet a glimmer of pride that I was following my dream even though I was scared. And in less than twenty-four hours it would be doomsday starting in my belly. *Diet.*

I paused mid-greasy fry and felt my cheeks lower. My biggest fear with dieting was losing the joyful opportunity to cook and bake. I loved being in the kitchen, making mouthwatering dinners and trying out new desserts, and a diet meant none of that, or at least not as much as I'd like. You didn't need to be a chef to make a salad.

Leaning my elbows on the table, I pondered everything in front of me like a movie. *This story follows a divorced thirty-nine-year-old woman taking on the hardest challenge of her life*, the voice-over would declare. *No, not chasing the dream of being an author. Chasing after the four-letter word* diet.

I sighed and shoved three fries into my mouth at once.

Chapter 4

My legs were Jell-O-like as I climbed from my Corolla in front of a blue sea-salt worn wooden sign with the words Cove Condos carved in white, stuck in the grass at the edge of the parking lot. The two-story building was a long rectangle. There was an office-like building in the middle. What it lacked in style and curb appeal, it made up for being directly on the beach and the insanely affordable price of rent for a year. It even had a bonus, it backed up to a cove, limiting traffic as the small-town restaurants and shops were about half a mile to the south.

The moist, salty air hit me before I could even see the water on the other side of the building. I touched the skin on my arm, as it was not used to anything but dry desert air. I could almost taste the salt on my tongue. Even though it was a beautiful sunny day, there was not another person in sight. The wind provided a chill that got under my clothes and seemed to sap any remaining heat from my bones.

I left everything but my purse in the car and searched on foot for condo number three, spotting it near the end on the right. Although it was a ground floor unit, the pictures showed it offered great eye-level views of the ocean just past the marshy landscape that held greenery threaded into the sand. The owner provided me with the code for the key holder that was hanging around the knob, and I pulled it up on my cell phone and punched it in.

Sliding the key into the lock, I squeezed my eyes shut because I hoped the owner hadn't misrepresented the condo in some bait and switch action. Maybe it reeked of smoke or things that were broken, bugs, or pet hair on every surface.

Oh, pets and their hair. Something I would never understand. How do people love their dogs and cats so much to put up with that?

I pushed the door open, and it didn't even squeak. Stepping forward, I crossed the doorway and was greeted by light all around. The stark white walls allowed the sun to bounce off the ocean's reflection and streamed in through the large patio slider, filling every corner of the condo. The front door bumped into the one and only bedroom to my left that was all white except for the blue curtains decorating the one high window. The mattress was, thankfully, free of stains. Directly in front of me was the bathroom that was right out of a La Quinta hotel: white tile, white shower, white sink, and white walls. For the first time, I was glad I'd bought those eggplant-purple bath towels and navy-blue sheets. They would add some much-needed color to the monochromatic condo.

I took a few steps back toward the front door, and to my right was a U-shaped kitchen with a 1990s white refrigerator, white gas stove, white microwave, and a small but sparkling stainless steel sink. The cabinets were honey-colored wood, and on top was old-school Venetian gold granite countertops. On the other side of the kitchen peninsula were two bar stools and a tan couch that faced the opposite wall with a fireplace and forty-inch TV hung above it. There wasn't a cable or satellite box, so it must be a smart

TV, which would allow for easy access to my streaming apps.

I walked toward the slider and glanced back at the bar stools. Oddly, if you eat there, your back was to the amazing view. I figured I'd do most of my salad eating on the couch or on the patio so I could see the ocean, not just hear it.

I removed the wooden dowel from the slider's track and slid it open. The scent of salty air and sound of birds greeted me as I stepped onto the patio. There was nothing but a thin and rusted metal-slatted guardrail around it, causing it to feel like you were invading your neighbors' privacy on both sides of you. But I was here to write, not be on *House Hunters*, so any design particulars about a home were temporary.

I returned inside and locked the sliding door. Although it was a nice seventy degrees, I didn't feel comfortable leaving the slider wide open while I moved my stuff from the car inside.

On my way back to the front door, I noticed a note on the kitchen counter that I'd missed.

Analena,

Welcome. I hope you enjoy your time here. If there are any issues, please reach out to me via email. It will be best with my schedule and lack of cell reception. Also, there is a building that, as you must have seen, is in the middle of a row of condos. Inside you'll find a small gym, a large assortment of paperback books in what they loosely refer to as "the library," although a poor excuse of one if you ask me, a pool table, and a large empty room to host birthday parties, etc. The second key on the key chain unlocks that building's door. Please make sure to lock up when you leave, or the condo board will have my head. The mailboxes are located on the north wall of the outside of that building. There is a playground just off the back as well, but I doubt you'll find a need for that. I wish I could tell you there is a swimming pool, but it would be unused with our weather. Besides, that's what the beach is for. Enjoy your year, and I hope you write the novel of your dreams.

Cathy

My stomach grumbled as I leaned over the peninsula, peering into the living room. The space was charming and cozy, even with the outdated kitchen, but there was something off; it lacked the personal touches that showcased a home's personality. It was as though Cathy didn't live here at all. I moved toward the wall, scanning for nail heads, assuming maybe she took down all her things to make it feel less like hers for the year. But there was nothing, and when I looked back at the refrigerator, there wasn't even a state-shaped refrigerator magnet. Thankfully, I had brought a box of personal favorites that included some framed pictures, a few candles, my hummingbird figurine knickknacks, my favorite purple quilt, and my white noise machine for the bedroom. My shoulders slumped and my back rounded into a slouch. How great could my life be if I could pack my most prized possessions into one box? "I guess less stuff for someone to sort through when I die."

Opening the cupboards one by one, I discovered that Cathy and I might have something in common. She had everything perfectly organized and the right amount of flatware and stemware—five each. She had every appliance available, including a Crockpot (*take that, Dawson*), an air fryer, a toaster, rice cooker, and pearl-white stand mixer. Then my mouth fell open, and I spun around.

"Oh my gosh." I took a deep breath.

She was missing one very, very important appliance. An appliance that every writer on the face of this earth needed. My hands found the counter, and I went back through every cabinet to make sure I'd not missed it. I had not.

"Where is the coffee maker?"

Coffee was life.

"Why would anyone not have a coffee maker? Even people who drink decaf have a bloody coffee maker!"

I pulled out my phone and searched for local stores. I was used to ordering every non-perishable item online, so I couldn't even think of where one might go to buy a coffee maker in the wild.

"Oh, they have Fred Meyer here." Spotting it on the map helped me recall I'd seen them on *Little People, Big World*, but Nevada didn't have one.

Removing my keys from my purse on the kitchen counter, I made my way to the Corolla and began unloading the car.

First, I brought in all the writer items, as they seemed the most valuable to me, then started lugging in my clothes.

"Hey, Gretel! You're leaving breadcrumbs."

I turned, balancing another pile of clothes across my arms. A woman about my age in a pink-and-yellow sundress with cropped bleached-blonde hair was holding a bag of . . . pellets. "Excuse me?"

She laughed and almost skipped in my direction. "Your clothes." She pointed behind me. "You've dropped a few, and it made me think of Hansel and Gretel."

"Oh!" I hurried to pick up the clothes, realizing they were my underwear and a bra. "Thank you." I shoved them inside the pile I was trying to balance.

She stood directly in front of me, and I noticed the letters on the bag of pellets spelled out Guinea Pig Food. *Oh no, a pet person.*

"I'm Piepie." She smiled, and I noticed she has the most perfectly straight teeth I'd ever seen.

I smiled in return but made sure my lips were covering my teeth, because I've never liked mine. My front teeth were angled slightly, and my eyeteeth were a little too pointy. "Hi, I'm Analena. I'm renting Cathy's place for the year."

Piepie tilted her head and glanced around the parking lot. "Cathy is nice and all, but we didn't get along too well, sort of glad she's gone. She isn't a fan of pets. And I have a lot." Piepie laughed. "Much to my husband's chagrin. But hey, he married me in sickness and health, and I need pets for my sanity, and that falls under health. Of course, Cathy said it's a sickness. Just because she's a doctor, she thinks she was always right and that there is such a thing as too many. People need pets, don't you agree?"

I blinked. "I think . . . that people . . . should do whatever makes them happy. I mean, chocolate cake is good, and you can't have too much of that?"

Piepie laughed and slapped my shoulder with her free hand. "You're funny, Analena. And I love it!" She switched the bag of guinea pig food to her other arm. "I think we're going to be good friends. But I must run. I'm late for my volunteer job at Coastal Rescue." She yanked a set of keys from her dress pocket. "Once you're settled in, let's plan a get-together. We can chat about life, and I'll make my famous chocolate martinis."

"That sounds like fun." The clothes were growing heavier in my arms, distracting me from making sure to check that we don't hang out at her condo for this get-together. I didn't know how many pets she had, but one was too many for me.

"Perfect. See you soon." Piepie turned and waved her hand up in the air as she made her way to a cypress gray Tahoe parked a few spots over.

After I unloaded my car, I made a grocery list on my phone so I wouldn't get distracted buying items I shouldn't with my new diet in play. Plus, I needed to stick to a menu every week, so I didn't waste food or money. I mean, what single person eats an entire heart of celery before it goes bad if not planned out for three separate meals? I had a nice stack of diet recipes saved on my Pinterest account, and I was determined to finally make a dent in the list. However, for tonight I would have a can of soup because who was I kidding? After a ten-hour drive, I just wanted to relax and take in the start of the fall weather.

"Actual fall weather," I said with a sigh as I opened the front door of the condo.

I shut the door and locked it, but when I spun around, I spotted a small dog, like the one Dorothy had in the *Wizard of Oz*, about three feet away. I backed into my front door, trying to avoid the little beast from getting any closer to me.

"Whoa, whoa, whoa. Dog, no, stay back. Back."

I glanced up to see that the dog's leash was held by a woman dressed in khakis and a blouse. She reminded me of Diane Keaton, only much older than in the '90s movies I remembered.

"Why, hello, I'm Janet." She shoved her left hand toward me. "You must be Cathy's long-term renter."

I glanced down at the white fur ball and then back up at Janet as the little thing sniffed my pant leg, causing my panic to grow deeper.

"I'm sorry." Janet wrapped the leash in her hand and then stooped to pick up the dog. "Are you afraid of dogs?"

"Yes." I made a pincer gasp with my fingers. "Just a little."

"Well, don't tell Piepie." She glanced over her shoulder, down the row of condos. "You don't have to worry about little Yo-Yo. She's curious but sweet and has never bitten anyone." Janet nestled her face into the dog's fur. "Although I've wanted her to a few times." She laughed and looked up. "Sorry, I don't recall Cathy telling me your name."

"Hi, yes, I am, I'm . . ." I went blank. "Analena. Sorry, it's been a long day."

"Nice to meet you, Analena. This is Yo-Yo."

I gave the dog a half-smile. "Hi, Yo-Yo."

"Yo-Yo the Yorkie." His tail thumped against Janet's arm. "Let me know if you need anything. Cathy told me you're writing a novel?"

"Yes, that's the plan anyway." I eyed Yo-Yo as though she might jump out of Janet's grasp like a flying squirrel and attack me.

"I don't think I could do with all the solitude writer's face. I'm a people person. Far too chatty to sit all day behind a desk and type. I did enough of that as a data entry clerk for forty-five years. Plus, with all the TV shows, when does anyone find time to read a book these days?"

I blinked.

"Oh, gosh"—her hand came out towards me—"that was not a very positive spin on what you're here to accomplish, now is it?" She waved her hand in the air. "Well, never mind me and my big mouth, making you feel like crap on your first day here." Janet glanced at Yo-Yo. "We're off for our evening walk. We aren't big on going after dark, so this time of year we do it before dinner."

Yo-Yo seemed to know what Janet was talking about as she wiggled her little body, and Janet set the dog down. I remained pushed up against the door, my feet scrunched back so far that my heels were touching the kickplate.

"See you around. I'm just next door if you ever need anything, give me a knock." Janet called over her shoulder as they exited the cover of the condo's upper balcony and headed around the building.

I glanced ahead but didn't see a single soul, although there were a handful of cars parked in the numbered spots. A breeze hit me when I made my way out of the cover of the building, and I shivered. At least soup would be the perfect dinner for tonight, hopefully masking the fact that it would not fill me up. This would be a very different fall, and a very different year than I was accustomed to, and both brought fear and excitement.

Chapter 5

Once I'd unloaded my groceries and the five-cup coffee maker was plugged in and ready for the following morning, I placed the potato soup in the microwave to heat it up. Outside, the sun was setting over the Pacific Ocean, and I didn't want to miss my first sunset in my new . . . gosh what was I to call this condo? Technically, it wasn't mine. I was only borrowing it, but it *was* where I'd be living for a year. I stared out the slider as the sky took on shades of orange sherbert. Home. Home is where you live, regardless of how long. Where you hang your hat, or purse, and where you create your dreams.

I took my amber ale beer with me to the slider, and exited onto the patio, zeroing in on the arching pastels over the water. Lowering into the woven wicker chair, I crossed my legs and rested the bottom of the bottle on my knee. Movement on a nearby balcony caught my attention.

"Beautiful sunset tonight," a male voice said from above me and over to my right.

"Yes. There is something surreal about it, as though there is emotion in the sun, and it's grateful for the respite in the calming ocean."

He leaned on the deck's railing, looking to the ocean, and I could just spot him when I leaned forward over my railing. "Or maybe sadness that another day is done."

The somberness of his comment caused me to pause. I couldn't make out his facial features to determine his age because of the strong reflection from the sun off the water.

"Either you broke into Cathy's place or you're her renter," he said.

"I hate to stop an intriguing criminal investigation, but I'm the renter." I looked up, holding his gaze.

"That's what a burglar would say to try to get out of being caught."

"Do I look like a burglar?"

"I don't associate with criminals, so I'm not sure."

"Neither do I, as I mentioned. I'm Analena. It's nice to meet you, I think."

"Todd." He raised the bottle he had in his hand, and I mirrored him with my beer.

I crossed my arms as a chill swirled in the air, the night growing cold instantly with the sun's last rays behind the water.

"I hope you brought enough warm clothes."

"I guess I'll find out." I laughed.

"Have a nice evening, possible burglar Analena."

"You too, suspicious Todd."

He gave a nod of his head, and I waved with my bottle, then headed inside to the beeping microwave. The scent of parsley, potatoes, and cheese filled my nose as I lowered the bowl with two oven mitts onto the counter.

There were only three soups I liked. Chicken noodle—*not* chicken and rice—tomato soup, and potato soup. I saw no reason for any other soups to be available on the market, least of all anything green, chunky, or spicy. Soup should be comforting, not a party invitation for salsa.

A loaf of store-bought sourdough sat on the cutting board, and I sliced off one piece, then stared at it for a few seconds and sliced another. I placed my not-really-diet-approved-bread next to the soup bowl and carried the meal into the living room and set them on the coffee table next to my also not-really-diet-approved beer. Tonight, I was celebrating the official start of my novel year, and thus I had a right to celebrate. I queued up *Capote* on the streaming app and tossed a pillow onto the floor. The coffee table would work until I could figure out a better way to use the bar stools at the peninsula so I could watch TV and the ocean instead of the refrigerator.

But I found I couldn't focus on the movie as my mind wandered. I'd seen it before but thought it would spark some extra creativity for my big first day of writing tomorrow. Really prepare my mind for writing.

I gazed around the living room. Where would I write?

There wasn't a desk in the bedroom, and the coffee table proved to be far too short for a good typing angle. Unlike a laptop, I couldn't rest the typewriter on my lap. I glanced over at the bar stools. I guess I could write there. It would allow me to keep from being distracted by the ocean view.

Exhaustion from the two days of driving caught up with me, and my eyelids grew heavy. I finished dinner, shut off the movie and decided on a quick shower. Returning, I spotted the moonlight bouncing off the ocean outside the slider and grabbed another beer from the refrigerator.

"Diets should never start on a Thursday anyways; that's a Monday thing."

A sense of peace that I had not felt in some time washed over me. Yet the peace was mixed with feelings of uncertainty. The path I was on had me standing at the starting line, and I didn't know how to get to the finish line, or if I could do it before time was up.

While my year off to write my novel was the main goal, deep down inside, I wanted to figure myself out. I needed to find out how I'd allowed myself to get off course and lose who I was prior to marrying Dawson. I had to discover why I'd allowed things in life to give me anxiety and depression. I needed to work on all levels of my health, both through exercise and eating. I had to dive deep into the truth of how I allowed life's ups and downs to sabotage me in little ways that added up. But I needed to let go of some beliefs about myself and my failed marriage. I wanted so much more from life than I'd given myself at this point. I wanted more meaning, prosperity, and joy.

I set my beer on the coffee table and grabbed my house sweater and keys. I headed out the front door, and the cold air brushed against my exposed skin like a dried paintbrush to a stiff and unyielding canvas. I followed a well-worn path running vertically along the back of the building, over the strip of wild grasses, and onto the beach.

My steps were fraught with loose sand, and the ocean mist dampened my parched Nevada hair. I made my way further down the shore with no idea of where I was going. With each step, I reveled in the fact that my dream was a reality. I was finally here. I might have been alone, but what a great accomplishment and privilege to be walking on the beach, just outside of my new home, on a chilly night. That was special. It was memorable. And tomorrow I'd start writing my novel.

My cell phone vibrated in my pocket, and I fished it out.

Dawson: Did you make it okay?

I let out a sigh.

"Too beautiful of a night to be checking that thing."

I let out a faint scream, and my cell crashed into the sand below.

"I'm sorry, I didn't mean to startle you," a man's voice filtered through the night air. "Is your phone alright?" He picked it up and handed it to me.

I looked over it, brushing off the sand. "Yeah." I pushed the side button, bringing it to life.

"It seems like those phones can take a lot, but they always manage to break on the least likely of drops." The man was in his late seventies and dressed in a thick jacket and wool ski hat.

I smirked.

"You must be freezing." He glanced at my sweater.

"I don't mind the freezing. It's sort of nice. I'm from Nevada."

"Ah, well, Nevada, I'm Mason, Mason Moore, I'm over at Cove Condos." He pointed with his head. "We don't get many out-of-towners at this end of the beach."

"I'm renting Cathy's condo for a year. But I'm sure I'll give off tourist vibes for a few months as I adjust."

"Sounds like an exciting year ahead for you, Nevada. Must be nice. No job?"

"I'm taking a sabbatical."

Mason breathed so deeply out his nose that I heard it over the ocean waves. "Hmm. You'll need some warmer clothes." He looked up at the moon.

"Yes, I might need to rethink some jacket options. I was just drawn to see the ocean up close. I'm sure the allure will wear off once I've been here a while."

"Don't bet on it. I've lived near the ocean my entire life, and it has yet to become less fascinating than the day I arrived. The only thing that is worn and uninteresting is me." He nodded his head toward the water, the foam rolling onto the shore. "I'm sure we'll see each other again, since you're not working."

I couldn't bring a smile to my lips. There was something about his demeanor towards me that shifted mid-conversation, and it wasn't pity.

"See you around." I watched Mason continue further down the beach, stability in his stride, like the bricks of a brownstone.

My phone vibrated again, alerting me to another text.

> Dawson: How does this big city feel so empty without you in it?

How dare he miss me? When we were married, he never did. I pondered my response as I made my way back to the condo. Thankfully, I had the moon's light to guide me as the outside lights of the condo building were as dim as a bathroom night-light.

But as I turned the key in the lock, it didn't feel like I was coming home. It was more like entering a hotel room as I shut the front door and removed my damp, sandy shoes. I glanced over at the bed and realized I had yet to throw my sheets on it. "Shoot."

I swiped the beer bottle off the coffee table and snuggled up with my fuzzy purple blanket to try to get some warmth back into my bones after the beach walk. I re-read Dawson's texts, unsure whether to respond. My best friend's voice came into my right ear as though she was the devil on my shoulder. *Don't do it. Don't you dare text him back.*

It's rude not to text back. He is only trying to be nice. I typed, deleted, typed again, deleted, typed.

> Analena: I made it. I don't know why you miss me. You have my Crockpot to keep you company.

Chapter 6

"What?" I blinked desperately trying to clear the fog of sleep from my vision as I stared at the cupboard.

I hurried to each cabinet and opened it up with both hands. "This can't be."

Every shelf in the entire condo had everything a kitchen needed, but mugs. Not a single coffee mug.

I scratched my head, my hand snagging on a night-time-produced knot from tossing and turning. How had I *not* noticed that when I first looked through the cupboards?

But it made sense. Cathy didn't have a coffee maker, or even a teakettle, so of course she wouldn't have mugs. I squinted. "Who is this monster?"

I scoped out the other cups and glasses and was not sure if I could use any of the delicate stemware as a mug. The hot coffee might crack them. I opened the cupboard, spotting the bowls. "Nope." I shook my head. "I'm not drinking out of that."

My vision traveled to the front door. "Janet," I whispered.

I threw on my sweater and headed outside, then knocked on my neighbor's door.

It eased open, and Janet appeared much more awake than I. "Good morning." She smiled as the scent of warm lavender and chamomile came wafting out from behind her.

"This is an odd request, but apparently Cathy doesn't have any mugs."

"Ahh, yes. She probably should've mentioned that." Yo-Yo squeezed between her legs.

I jumped back, clasping my hands together.

"Sorry, forgot." Janet scooped up Yo-Yo.

"Can I borrow a mug from you? I'm in desperate need."

Her smile faded, and she pet Yo-Yo's head hard enough that her eyes seemed to be pulled up and back as though preparing for a K-9 nip-tuck. "See, here's the issue. I only have three, and they're very special to me—gifts from my grandchildren—so I can't part with them, even for a neighbor."

"Oh." I wrapped my sweater tighter and bit my lower lip. "Um, okay, sorry to have bugged you."

"If you need anything else, let me know." Janet moved back inside her condo.

"Just not the mugs," I sighed.

"Have a good day...?"

"Analena."

"Sorry, I forgot." Janet nodded. "Analena."

She eased the door closed, and I heard her slide the lock back into place. I didn't bring my favorite mug or even a special mug, although I knew it was a very big thing for authors, and now, I was doubting if I was starting off on the wrong foot on day one. Hopefully, this wasn't some sort of sign.

"Morning!" a man's voice called as I heard his shoes reach the bottom step.

I recognized his voice from yesterday, but his face, I'd not seen. And now I wish I had because I'm pretty sure my mouth was hanging open. I was not prepared for *this*. He was bald but a good-looking bald, like Jason Statham.

"You're?" I pointed my finger at him and then up to the second level.

"Suspicious Todd."

"You're chipper for so early in the morning." I made sure my sweater was wrapped completely over my pajamas.

"Ah, possible burglar Analena." He was standing in front of me, dressed in a heavy green Carhartt jacket and blue jeans. I looked up because he was massively tall. Even though I'm short, he still seemed taller than normal tall. And his nose was just the cutest thing.

"How short are you?" Todd asked, peering down.

"That seems really forward." I squinted at him.

"No, measuring you would be forward." He removed a metal tape measure from the back pocket of his jeans and extended the tape, the metal hook tapping the ground.

"You know they sell tape measures from the current century." I laughed. "Four eleven."

"I would have guessed five one." Todd retracted the tape back into the holder. The noise sounded like a slithering snake, then halted as it stuck midway. He wiggled it, and then it shot up, winding all the way. He clipped the tape measure back onto his pocket.

"How tall are you?" I craned my neck.

"Six three."

"Why are you so happy, six-three Todd? Is it because you're closer to the sunshine?"

He laughed, and it was a cute laugh. How does a man who looks like he walked off a movie set where he lifted weights for eight hours laugh like he's your childhood friend who could do no wrong?

"Why not be happy in the morning? I got to sleep in today, late start at work." He held a stainless-steel coffee mug and keys in his right hand.

"I see you have coffee?" I leaned forward.

"Yes?" Todd glanced at his mug and then at me.

"Do you have a coffee mug that I can borrow? For a day or two at the most, until I can make it to the store."

He nodded his head. "Cathy and her no-coffee life. Very odd." His forehead wrinkled.

"Right!" I held back my hand that wanted to slap him on the arm in agreement.

"Plus, Janet and her no-loan rule." Todd jogged up the stairs, and I heard keys. "Hang on, and I'll grab you one."

Wrapping myself tighter in my sweater, I watched my breath in the air, and it was rather mesmerizing. Because of the dry air in Nevada, it was a rare thing to see this happen.

"I hope this is to your liking?" Todd held out a navy-blue mug with white writing.

"Thank you." I took it from him and read it Best Dad Evfur.

I glanced at Todd and then back at the mug.

"Sorry, it might have dog hair in it. It's everywhere."

"Oh, I get it; instead of *ever* it's *evfur*." I peer into the mug but, thankfully, don't see any dog hair. "Was this a gift?"

"No."

"So, you're a dog dad and think you're the best?"

"Whidbey sure thinks so. You'll meet him soon. Anyways, I better get to work."

"Sorry to keep you, and thank you again." I turned towards my front door. "Have a good day at work."

He headed to his truck. "Thanks, you too."

I waved his mug at him, headed inside, and shut the door. When my forehead found the back of the door's cool wood, I rested it on it. Todd was handsome, ruggedly handsome, like he could protect you from danger but also save a cat stuck on a roof. But he had a dog. This place was turning into a zoo. Did everyone have animals? When I thought about it, it was a good thing that he had a dog. I didn't need any romantic distractions, especially with someone who could be Jason Statham's twin brother. Todd will be an attractive neighbor and nothing more; no friendship, just neighbors who borrow kitchen items, with an occasional wish that he takes his shirt off. No harm in that. I'm sure he'll get hot in the summer. I was here to focus my sights on writing and away from the sight of Todd. Besides, someone who looks like him can't be single. I sighed as I slid the mug under the coffee maker and punched the power button.

My first day of writing was a mix of excitement and hesitation. With my steaming mug of coffee, I made my way to the slider, then remembered how cold it was outside and opted to sit on the couch. I couldn't wait to use the fireplace, and judging by the temperatures so far, it would be soon. The way the dampness got to your bones here was a novel experience for me. The thermostat was set at sixty-eight, but it felt like fifty-eight.

I leaned back into the plush couch pillows and took a short sip of coffee, unsure of its temperature. My hands wrapped around the entire mug, absorbing the heat through the porcelain. I glanced at the typewriter on the peninsula; something was holding me back. I may not be a published author, but I knew starting was the hardest part. I had my novel's outline, a notebook full of plot points, character names and profiles, and story arcs, but that didn't make for an instant easy dive. In fact, I was not even sure how well everything would weave together. I'd changed the ending three times on my outline.

With my socked feet pressed up against the coffee table, I picked up my phone and scrolled through the two social media sites I had a profile on. One author I followed posted a photo of her fall coffee mug next to her laptop with the view of her office muted in the background. Another author had posted a video of her unboxing her latest book, and jealously coursed through me. A friend from high school had posted photos of their beach vacation with her beautiful family, and there was a new post from several accounts I followed that had writing tips and tricks.

Then there was my account. The last two pictures I posted were of my final townhome macaroni and cheese dinner. The other was of all my writing items stacked high in my Corolla. Four likes for one, five for the other, and not a single comment. I scrolled back up to the authors' posts and noticed hundreds of likes and comments. I wanted people to be curious about me. I wanted them to have a desire to get an insider's look into the writer behind the story, from start to finish. I wanted to make friends with those who followed me, and I wanted to inspire them in their lives to follow their dreams. But at this point, I was just another profile among millions of others.

I pushed past the self-doubt, stood up and took Todd's mug over to the typewriter on the peninsula, setting it off to the right, my notebooks sat on the left. Snapping a picture of myself leaning up against the typewriter, I posted it with the caption First Day of My Novel Year. Maybe a little dramatic, but I'm a writer, and every good story had some form of drama in it.

After I finished my coffee, I pulled on jeans and my favorite blue sweater, hoping it would make me feel more ready to tackle the writing as though it were my job. The condo had only two mirrors, one in the bathroom and one in the bedroom; neither allowed me to see below my bra line. Which could be seen as helpful or harmful, I'd figure that out later. I pulled out my eating journal and scribbled last night's soup and bread, and two bottles of beer. Then I added the coffee, even though it was something silly like two calories. I closed the journal, feeling as though I was off to a good start by tracking my calories and the rest would fall into place, at least I hoped.

Topping off my coffee, I slid onto the bar stool and threaded a sheet of clean white paper into the lateral paper guide, turning the platen knob on the left and making sure it fed up and under the card holder. Excitement and hesitation built up inside of me. It was finally happening, the big D R E A M. But what if I couldn't do it? No, of course I could. It was my destiny. I began to type.

HARBOR HILLS

Home Sinful Home

by

Analena McCoy

Draft 1

I pulled the page from the typewriter, but when I held it up, the typing was slightly blurry and slanted at least five degrees downward and to the right. "Dang, good thing it's just a first draft." I set the title page upside down to my right, then added a new sheet, double-checking the straightness before snapping the paper bail into place.

A smile crossed my lips as I opened my outline notebook. I took a sip of coffee and rested my fingers on the bulky keys.

Chapter 7

My fingers were still resting on the keys of the typewriter a few minutes later, having yet to type anything other than the chapter heading. The wooden bar stool was uncomfortable even with the small seat cushion tied to the spindles.

"Okay, the opening sentence needs to be catchy." I wiggled my fingers as they tapped the keys like a pretend Little Tikes toy piano. I'd not done much typing since high school, and my skills were rusty. I looked down at the keys. It would be a slow process until I could get my typing speed and accuracy up to par.

"Just start typing." I pulled my shoulders back and pressed into the keys.

```
It started with a gun. It ended with
   a gun. But it was what happened in
            between that mattered.
```

I crossed my arms, shook my head, and yanked the paper out. Then, I added a new sheet and lined it up.

```
    I want his head brought to me in a
   nice cardboard box, set on my front
doorstep. I want to open the door and
  look down and see a brown box, with
```

```
the lid folded over, so it doesn't
  flap in the wind. I'll bend over,
unfold the box's lid and there he'll
be. His head looking right up at me.
Of course, that's not how it happened.
Life doesn't always go as planned. For
  Joan, it went so vastly different.
```

I took a long sip of coffee, wishing it were a cabernet, then pulled the sheet of paper out and added a new one.

```
It was not that I didn't hear the
scream. More that it could've belonged
  to a female . . . or a peacock. My
house backed up to an old farmstead
  that had over thirty beautiful but
  seemingly disgruntled birds, whose
calls sounded like a person screaming.
```

I scooted back on the stool and stretched my arms wide, arching my back in relief. I had to write at least one page of my story. One can't edit a blank page. But I had to decide which opening I liked best, if any at all. I read back through the three opening lines I'd typed, finally deciding on one after three sips of coffee and fed it back through the paper guide to add the next paragraph.

"One paragraph at a time," I reminded myself, resting my fingers back over the keys.

I checked the clock on the stove; it was just after ten. If most authors write two thousand words a day, I could easily write a page or two. My stomach grumbled, and I craved a blueberry muffin with crumble topping. Glancing over at my diet journal, I groaned. Heading to the refrigerator, I removed the Greek yogurt and fresh blueberries and swiped the granola from the counter. That would have to do. I made myself a late breakfast, hoping the healthy fuel would kick a few pages into drive when I returned to the typewriter.

But I sat there, staring at it. What was I thinking? Write a book? I can't do that. *No. Stop it. I can write a book. Focus.*

Once the yogurt got to my stomach and worked its way into whatever it works into, I'll be set. To be honest, it was probably my writing area. I needed a desk or something that I could use as a desk.

After finishing breakfast, I forced my fingers back onto the keys. The words turned into sentences and then into paragraphs as I worked on the story, stopping to check my notebooks to refresh my memory on the characters' traits. The typewriter was new enough that it had the ability to erase, but I still needed to be careful since I couldn't do it as easily or as much as if I were on a computer. But after an hour, the words slowed from a tortoise to a snail's pace. I stood up, gripping the counter's edge. My bottom had fallen asleep, and my legs and back were sore. "Yeah, this writing setup is not going to work."

The clock on the stove read three in the afternoon. I'd missed lunch, which was probably a good thing, but I'd also spent about five hours with little writing to show for it. I needed to stretch my legs and see what the so-called gym looked like.

I double-checked that there was an extra key on the key chain per Cathy's note, changed into exercise clothes, and headed over.

The parking lot held only a few cars, including mine, and I unlocked the community center door. Directly in front of me, two bookcases flanked the windows, shoved full of paperback and hardcover books. To the right, farther inside, were a pool table and fireplace with a beaten-up floral-print couch from the late nineties with wood trim. To the left was a gym, separated by glass walls and a door. Inside the gym, a woman was lifting weights while a man ran on the treadmill. The man looked familiar; it was the older man from the beach. I gave a wave. When the man caught sight of me, he did a half-hearted wave, and his mouth moved. The woman with him reacted to whatever he said by glancing over at me. I waved again, and the woman gave the same half-hearted wave.

Good thing there were miles of beach just outside my patio and walking was the easiest way to kick-start my fitness routine. I was no longer going inside a gym with two residents who didn't know me and clearly didn't like me. Heading back to the bookcases, I began reading the titles, feeling self-conscious about mine; it no longer sounded as catchy as I thought.

I wasn't sure how many minutes I'd been zoned out on the book titles when a blast of cool air rushed up behind me. I turned and saw a figure coming through the door, bald and rugged. *Ah, Todd.*

"Twice in one day." He stopped in front of me, dressed in gym shorts and a T-shirt. His arms were bulky, as though he was smuggling condensed chicken noodle soup cans in his biceps.

"Hi, yes."

"Looking for something in particular?" Todd pointed at the bookcase behind me.

I turned around as though I had forgotten what I had just been doing. "Yes, I'm ... well ... I needed to get up and move around, and wanted to check out the gym, and now I'm looking at book titles." I paused, bit the inside of my cheek. "See, I'm working on ... this is research ... I have a manuscript. It has a title. I'm writing a book. Or trying too."

"Nice."

"Nice?" I tilted my head, gazing up at him.

"No, it's bad?" Todd flipped the keys in his hand.

"Sorry, I guess I was expecting a different response."

He nodded. "You don't look like you're dressed to be a writer. Shouldn't you be wearing a bathrobe, with your hair all askew?"

"Wow." My head pulled back. "That's pretty stereotypical of you."

"I've seen it on TV and in movies. Of which there are many." He smirked.

"I can tell you those are inaccurate. And I've gone old school. I'm on a typewriter."

"Like Jessica Fletcher?"

I smiled and rocked on the balls of my feet. "That's me."

"No, that's Jessica Fletcher, you're Analena . . . something." He crossed his arms over his chest, causing his muscles to flex.

"McCoy. Analena McCoy. And I was going distraction-free for the novel writing, no internet."

"Brave move, Ms. Analena McCoy. Why not go to the local library? You can use something that doesn't have access to all your personal stuff, and you can be current in this decade. Besides, you have a cell to distract you, and don't you need the internet for research?"

"I'm not writing nonfiction, so not too much research. I'm actually pretty good at ignoring my cell phone. And I was really hoping to write and live in the same spot, so the library wasn't on my list for places to compose a novel. I want to see the ocean, hear it, and smell it too. But I'm sort of stuck because I was expecting the condo to have a desk. Who doesn't have a desk?"

"I don't." His eyes squinted.

"You and the doctor are odd."

"What about your desk back home?"

"Didn't fit in my Corolla." I frowned. "I was thinking I could use the peninsula in the kitchen, but it's not working."

"Will it work for a few more days?"

I played with the key ring in my hand, rubbing my thumb on the bumpy key. "It's going to have to."

"I can build you something. Most of what you can buy is expensive or poorly made. But I'd need a few days."

"You'd do that?"

"Why not? You need a desk, and there is scrap wood all over my job sites, and I hate seeing it go to waste."

"I can pay you, but not much."

He stretched his right hand up to scratch at the back of his neck and his tricep flexed. I felt rouge race up my neck to my face. "How about this? Christmas is right around the corner, and I have a mom and sister that I can never seem to shop for. You help me figure out gifts for them and we'll call it even." He shoved his right hand in my direction.

I shook it. His fingers were rough, and his palms calloused, but he was gentle when he gripped my hand. "Okay, that would be absolutely amazing. Thank you."

"Great, I'm off to go work out." He directed his head with a nod toward the gym area and began walking that way.

"Be careful. Those two in there don't seem to like me, and they don't even know me."

Todd paused and looked over his shoulder at me. "Mason and Debbie?"

"I met Mason last night on the beach. But I don't know Debbie. Either way, it's polite to give a decent wave."

"I wasn't aware there were levels of waving." Todd glanced at me and then at the gym. "Mason thinks us youngsters don't do anything of value."

"I mentioned I wasn't working."

Todd nodded. "That'll do it." He stepped back towards me. "Don't let him get to you, or his wife, Debbie. It's none of his business what you or anyone else does. It's not like he's collecting mortgage payments around here."

I crossed my arms over my chest but knew it wouldn't be so easy for me to forget someone's unwarranted distaste for me.

Todd cleared his throat. "I knew I needed to know your height this morning. We just didn't know why yet."

"How so?" I question where Todd is going with this.

"I need to make the desk fit you so that you can type properly. There is no point in making a desk where you look like a nosy neighbor peeking over the fence trying to type."

"Good call, I'd prefer not to be Wilson. Thank you, Todd."

"*Home Improvement.*" He laughed and headed toward the gym and gave a wave over his shoulder. "And my pleasure."

Against my will, I selected a few novels from the book-case, even though I try to only read classics, and hurried back to my home, texting my best friend along the way.

> Analena: My desk issues are solved. My neighbor is building me a desk.

> Amy: Fancy and so sweet. Does the neighbor have a name?

> Analena: Yes, he does, but I'm not telling you.

> Amy: Remember, you're there to do more than write a book. You're there to rediscover yourself and open up to new opportunities.

> Analena: The only opportunity I'm here for is trying to figure out how to procure a calorie-free cake and ice cream.

I set my phone next to the typewriter as something in me sparked. I put a new sheet of paper into the typewriter, and my fingers instantly went to work.

```
It took place the evening of July 4.
The weapon fired, but the gunshot was
masked by fireworks going off in the
street. Ms. Joan Whimpal, 78, careful-
```

ly unwrapped her chocolate ice cream
bar, being sure as to not drip any of
it on the man that lay dead next to
her wheelchair. With some careful work
around the house, the cops would call
this one what it wasn't, a burglary.

Chapter 8

There was a knock on my door as the oven timer went off. I assumed it was Todd, needing to measure something for the desk. But when I opened it, Janet was standing there, thankfully without Yo-Yo.

"Hi, Analena." She held up a fall-inspired coffee mug. "Rental condo-warming gift?"

I took the cute little mug of brown, orange, and yellow that said FALL in a leaf pattern on it. Warm feelings of nostalgia circled inside of me. It looked so '90s. "Thank you. It's adorable."

"I didn't mean to be rude earlier, but I was. I'm sentimental about memories with my kids. They live all the way out in South Carolina, and I see them once a year, at best. Anyways. Have a nice evening."

"Do you want to join me?" I asked.

She gave me a look that I could only take as surprise. Surprised that she'd been invited, mixed with joy. "Oh, I can't intrude."

"On my lavish party?" I held the door wide open. "I've been making kale chips. I love to bake, but it turns out that when you're on a diet, making cookies and cupcakes is frowned upon. I also made some granola bars."

Janet checked her wristwatch. "It's suppertime. You can't eat granola and kale for a meal."

"You're right, I was going to have soup for dinner."

"Soup? Well, how about that! I just made a fresh loaf of sourdough bread." Janet clapped her hands together. "I'll be right back."

I winced, looking at the soup cans. I should have bought the ingredients to make it from scratch; it would have tasted better, but I wasn't planning on company. Plus, soup two nights in a row was already getting tiresome. While it was healthier than mac and cheese and lower in calories, it wasn't if I added bread. So much for that. *There's always tomorrow.*

Janet and I decided to sit at the peninsula, basically because it was the only place to sit with soup. I was okay with not watching the beautiful view out the window because I craved someone to chat with. I'd missed the daily conversations at my job back in Nevada. Speaking with customers provided a steady stream of brief conversations at my register. Many of the regulars picked my line so they could fill me in on the prior week's happenings, or so I could hand out stickers to their kids who I knew by name. Plus, I'd not been speaking as much with Amy as I'd assumed I would. For one reason or another, our contact was slipping. From what I understood, being an author was a very lonely profession, and some were okay and even thrived in solidarity. However, at this point, I was not one of them.

"Now, remind me, you're writing a novel?" Janet asked, blowing on the spoonful of chicken noodle soup.

"I think it's fair to say I'm attempting to write a novel. The first day is in the bag, but it was not what I expected. I guess I thought it would be easier since it's been my dream for so long. While energy itches at my fingers and creativity flowed from me when I got down to writing, it was as though I'd started in the middle of a subpar book."

"Yes, saggy middle syndrome."

I laughed. "I feel like I should see my OBGYN for that."

"Don't get me started on menopause, we'd need another loaf of bread to soak that all up."

"I'm experiencing the joys of perimenopause." I sighed. "Not something I get excited to talk about. So tell me, I bet you have a bucket list?"

"I think writing a book is far different from showing up to swim with dolphins." Janet slurped her soup. "Besides my bucket list is long gone."

"You can't disregard your dreams." I tore off a piece of Janet's sourdough bread that was so moist and soft it nearly melted between my fingers. "So, swimming with dolphins is one of them?"

"I have a long list of dreams. But my social security budget doesn't allow for such endeavors. I don't mean to sound negative, but at my age, the facts are the facts. I can only wish upon the stars that someday I'll be able to buy a house, have a small yard for Yo-Yo to run around in. And yes, swim with dolphins."

"That makes me sad. I feel bad I have the opportunity to chase mine."

"Don't be. I've lived a great life, and I've done far more than I ever thought I would. I guess as I got older, my priorities shifted because I changed and the world changed. I didn't count on my husband of thirty-eight years cheating on me. I didn't count on my children moving to the East Coast. For now, I'm trying to figure out, yes even at my age, what I want to do with the rest of my life, because each day is a gift but also a day closer to the end."

"That must be difficult. Although I don't think you're old, just older than me. And I must say, this bread is amazing. I'm disappointed you don't have a dream about opening a bakery." I took another bite.

"Thank you. Baking is a hobby, something fun that has a tasty reward. My genuine passion is making stained glass, the small ones. The kind you can hang from your window, nothing bigger than twelve-by-twelve inches."

"That's amazing. I'd love to see some of your pieces."

"And I'd be happy to show you."

"I'd like that. I guess the whole author dream feels odd now that it's happening because I'm at the beginning, yet I feel distant from it. As though I'm unsure of my decision."

"If I could go back and redo areas of my life, I would. Including not marrying husband number one or two."

"Really, neither of the two marriages were good?"

"Correct. Have you been married?"

"Long enough to be divorced." I took another bite of the soup. It was cooling down quickly with all the chatting.

"Ah, welcome. It's a great club, once you figure out how to live life in a new way." Janet clasped her hands together over the bowl.

"How about some wine?" I set my spoon down.

"I thought you'd never ask." Janet smiled.

After I opened the cabernet, our conversation grew deeper, more emotional, totally unexpected. I was sucked into Janet's story about her marriages, having kids, the one divorce and the second after discovering the affair. It made me grateful, for the first time, that Dawson and I divorced over lack of communication and turning out to be very different people with different goals. I was thankful I didn't have to deal with the effects of an affair. I think that would have ruined any part of my heart that still had hope about finding and holding onto love.

Thankfully, but not for my waist, Janet left the rest of the sourdough loaf with me. And I used it to soak up the cabernet in my stomach that had made me rather tipsy. I was not looking forward to writing in my food journal tonight.

Taking a slice of bread and my half glass of wine, I exited onto the patio and curled up in the single patio chair. The cold night's air felt refreshing on my alcohol-warmed cheeks. Muted lights from the sliders up and down the condo's backside provided a soft glow onto the beach.

The waves crashed in the distance, and the moon's light acted like a night-light on the surface of the water and across the sand. Everything Janet had said ran back through my mind. For the first time, I gave real thoughts to my divorce and myself. After all, when you had conversations in your head, there was no one else to judge you; you could be as honest as you wanted. A part of me wasn't sure what the truth really was. Sure, Dawson and I'd grown apart from all the differences, but also it felt like we'd fallen out of love because we lacked the communication to fix it. I began to enjoy hanging out with my friends more than with my husband. In those times, we grew and changed into different people. Priorities shifted, and getting home from work was not the happy time it once was. It turned into a chore. All the little things he did that I sort of looked past for years started to drive me nuts. The way he laughed, the way he blew his nose, how he fluffed his pillow like it was a punching bag; how he left his socks—nothing else, just his socks—on the floor. I could never figure out how he managed to put all his clothes in the hamper but miss the socks.

I needed my phone, so I headed back inside. I set the wineglass on the coffee table and munched on the remaining piece of sourdough bread, pulling up Dawson's number.

He answered on the third ring. "Analena, surprised to hear from you after your snippy text."

"Don't be too surprised. I have a question that needs answering, buddy." *Gosh, whenever I drink too much, all men's names turn into* buddy.

"Are you drunk?"

"No-ish, the best bread I've ever had is soaking up the extra wine I shouldn't have had. Now, don't distract me. I called because I wanted to know why you always left your socks all over the place?"

"My socks? You're calling to ask about my socks?"

"Look here, buddy. You went through more socks than toilet paper in a day, and then you would leave them all over the place. Used socks!"

"My feet sweat a lot, you know that. I had to change them often."

"It defeats the point of having no stink in the house if you just leave the stink all over the place. You wrap that up and shove it in the bottom of the hamper. It drove me so batty that you did that. And you know what else?"

"Not really."

"You didn't cheat on me, and while I appreciate that, you didn't love me hard enough. You should have loved me harder, like a rock." I shook my head and took another sip of wine. "No, not a rock, you should have loved me like a boulder. But you gave all your love to your friends. Your friends always came first. You cared more about them than me. I deserved better."

"You're right."

I blinked, my vision fuzzy. "You're what?"

"You're right. I have regrets, and that is why I want to try to see if we can work it out. But all you want to do is move on and live in some fantasy writing land."

"It's not a fantasy. It's reality, buddy." I pulled the phone away from my ear and hit End. Then I hit it again a few more times for good measure.

I didn't even realize I was crying until a tear ran down my chin and onto my neck. I wrapped myself tighter in my house sweater and continued to cry, feeling sorry for myself and my life. This is not how my novel year was supposed to start.

Chapter 9

It'd been two days since I last saw Todd, which was a good thing. While I needed and wanted my desk, I also didn't need his face—or his tall and strong body—distracting me. The thing about being a writer is you can be a hermit, and no one bats an eye. There were three chapters sitting stacked to the right of my typewriter when my cell phone alerted me to a text.

> Amy: Has Tape Measure Man been by with your desk yet?

> Analena: You must be reading my mind. I was just thinking about that.

> Amy: About the desk or the man?

I held my phone in both hands, reminding myself to be careful how I answered.

> Analena: The desk, of course.

There was a knock at the front door, and I set my phone down to answer it. I pulled the door open to find Todd standing there.

"Speak of the devil." I placed my hands on my hips.

"No, it's Todd. T-O-D-D. For a writer, I expected more from you." He wore his green Carhartt jacket and jeans that looked like they needed a wash . . . and a prewash soak.

"Funny, I thought you spelled Todd P-O-M-P-O-U-S."

"My mom named me. Take it up with her." He chuckled. "I've got your desk. Can you help me grab it from my truck?"

"I can try." I wrangled my boots on over my fussy socks and followed him into the parking lot.

He pulled the tarp off the truck bed, revealing four legs sticking up like a dead cockroach. I really needed to remember to research why all dead cockroaches always went upside down.

"It looks fantastic, thank you." I peered towards the tailgate.

"You can't even see the top yet. I hope you like it." He shoved the tarp near the back of the bed and then hopped down. "You stand opposite, and we can slide it out on the blanket and then flip it over."

We worked together as though this was our hundredth time unloading a desk. Maybe in a different life we owned a moving company together. The teamwork was seamless, with no hostility in the other person's abilities or lack of communication, and it perplexed me since every time Dawson and I had to do a team activity it usually involved him getting grumpy and me stubbing a toe.

Once inside the condo, Todd and I set it down in front of the fireplace. I ran my hand over the slats of wood, the grain unmatched but somehow perfectly blended. "This is such a beautiful desk. The wood is too pretty to set a typewriter on."

"That'll make typing a challenge."

"What type of wood is this?"

"You've got a mix of oak, ash, and beech." Todd leaned his arm on the top of the bar stool seat.

"And they had this all at your worksite? What is it you do?"

"I'm a roofer."

"This doesn't look like roof wood."

"My dog thinks so, it's real *woof* wood." He glanced down at the floor and then back at me.

"Funny. But seriously, this is far from plywood."

"You needed a desk, now you have one, shorty."

"Hey, don't call me short."

"Well, I can't call you tall. That wouldn't make any sense."

I gasped and placed my hand on my forehead. "I don't have a chair." I glanced around the living room as though I had misplaced it.

"Yes, you do." Todd pointed toward the patio.

"That's a patio chair. It's outside."

"Hence the name." Todd went to the slider and unlocked it, sliding it open. "This will work great."

"Until I get a new chair."

Todd carried the chair inside and set it down. "Until you get an official office chair. So, where are we putting the desk?"

I glanced around the small living room. The only place to put it was in the middle of the room and in the middle of the way, in front of the fireplace or in front of the slider. "Let's go with in front of the slider. It blocks some of the view when you're not writing, but not too much, plus what a view for when you're typing away."

We moved the desk into position, and Todd set the patio chair in front of it. "Let's see how I did." He pointed to the chair.

I glided into the seat and scooched myself into position. He moved behind me, returning with my typewriter, setting it in front of me. I make a slight adjustment and set my hands on the keys. "This is perfect. Thank you so much." Turning to smile at him, I'm blinded by a flash. "What is happening?" My hand covered my eyes as I saw the blue spots fading.

"I took a photo. You've never had a picture taken before?"

"Of course I have." I stand up, regaining my vision. "But who uses a flash these days?"

Todd looked at his cell phone and then back at me. "It takes a clearer picture. It's cloudy out."

"We're inside."

Todd glanced around. "You need to turn on some lights. It's not good for your eyes to type in the dark."

"You're so very helpful." I pushed him towards the front door. "And it's plenty bright in here. The stark white walls reflect light like Grandma's polished silver."

When he resisted, his back muscles pressed into my palms, and I dropped my hands from his jacket as if it was on fire. *Why am I touching him?*

"I should get back to Whidbey." Todd spun around at the front door. "Are you sure you like the desk?"

I glanced back over my shoulder at it. "I love it, thank you. I look forward to helping you shop for your family."

"Just you wait. You won't be." He stepped outside onto the welcome mat.

"It won't be bad, I promise."

"I'll hold you to that." Todd shoved his hands into his jeans pockets. "How's the writing going?"

"It's going, just not sure where it's going. Some keys have been sticking, and the knob on the right gets jammed from time to time. But the desk will be a great help. I was getting all cramped up trying to type at such a high angle."

"I'm glad. If you ever need to get out and stretch your legs, I walk Whidbey twice a day."

I shook my head. "Thank you, but I don't really do pets."

Todd leaned so far forward my hands went out, thinking he was going to fall into me. "I'm sorry. I think I misheard you."

"You didn't. I'm not a fan of animals, pets, cats . . . dogs."

Todd's mouth hung open. His eyes searched around, lost. "At all? Not even cute puppies?"

I shook my head.

"But everything is better with a dog."

"Sorry." I rested my hand on the inside doorknob.

"Oh, no. No sorry here, we'll be fixing that."

"Fixing what?"

"You."

"I'm not broken."

"You're petrified. Literally, *pet*-rified." Todd walked backward toward the stairs. "I'll have you loving dogs before your year is up."

"Impossible."

"Challenge accepted." He turned around and jogged up the rest of the stairs.

I exited my condo. "It wasn't a challenge!" I glanced up at the balcony as I heard his door open and shut. "Drat."

Chapter 10

Over the last week, when I went for walks or to the library, I'd not seen Todd or his truck. Which was a good thing, I reminded myself, because I'd also not had him force any of his pet plans on me. But in the meantime, the residents had added Halloween décor to their front doors, and some condos on the second level had skeletons hanging along their balconies with black-and-orange lights.

I was typing away when a loud knock at my door caused me to hit several incorrect keys right at an important part of the scene I'd been trying to figure out for the last two hours. "Grr!"

I sauntered to the front door and eased it open.

"Analena, is it true?" Piepie was standing outside the front door, and in her hands was a creature, one that looked just like the one on the bag of pellets. It was a guinea pig.

I stepped back, using the door as a possible flying guinea pig barrier. "Is what true?"

"You don't like animals?"

I pinched my lips together. "I'm not a fan. I don't aspire to be around them. They should all live in the wild, not with people."

Piepie's mouth was hanging so far open I could see her molars, and I was afraid she'd drop the burrito-wrapped rodent. Several seconds passed, and I waved my hand in front of her because she wasn't blinking.

She finally blinked. "Analena, pets need people. People need pets. Just like Nellie here." She held up the fuzzy black-and-white ball. Its mouth twitched and opened as though it was going to start giving me grief, and I leaned back farther. "Do you think my guinea pigs could live freely in the wild? No, the answer is no, they could not. Can my little sweet Valentino and my spunky Marshall live in the wild? No, Analena, the answer is no to all." Piepie reached inside and took my hand. "Did something happen to you in your childhood that made you this way? Did a dog bite you?" She patted the top of my right hand as I glanced down at it and then back up at her.

"No." I shook my head. "I've never had a pet and . . . I think they're . . . scary." Piepie squeezed my hand tighter. "Plus, they make a mess—their hair, fur, is everywhere." I pulled my hand from hers. "Who told you about this?"

"Todd, he said I needed to know as part of his two-pronged plan." Piepie smiled.

"Of course he did."

"We still need to have a girls get-together, just the two of us. When are you free?" She leaned forward a smidge and peeked around me, as though there was a calendar on the wall behind me.

I leaned back as Nellie the guinea pig got closer. "I'm not sure. This manuscript is taking a lot longer than I imagined."

"Writers need breaks. How about now?"

I looked at my desk, then back at Piepie, who was doing a great job of looking needy and sad simultaneously. Which was odd because she was a walking joy emoji every other time I saw her.

"Sure, now is okay." I pointed at her guinea pig. "That's *not* invited."

Piepie's shoulders rose, and she turned toward her condo. "No worries, Nellie can't hold her bladder too long, anyway."

Piepie returned in a matter of minutes as I stood at the open door. She spotted me and brought her hands together as if she were about to pray but rubbed them with a grin. She would've looked like an evil dictator hatching a plan if it weren't for her sweater that read *Hold on, I see a guinea pig.*

I stepped aside and ushered her in. "Can I get you something to drink?"

"Is it too early for a cocktail?" She looked at her cell phone.

The clock on the stove read 2:49. "I don't think so."

"Oh, wait!" Piepie froze. "I need to make my chocolate martinis." She was at the door before I could answer and returned just as fast with a basket full of drink ingredients.

"Have you ever thought about the word *cocktail*? It sounds like something a peacock would come up with, you know, if they could talk. 'Hi, I'm a peacock. I'm fancy when I aspire to be. Let's have a cocktail.'" Piepie laughed and stood at the counter, pulling what she needed from the basket. "Or maybe a cockatiel. A cocktail for a cockatiel."

I leaned on the countertop and laughed.

Piepie began mixing like she was a bartender. "I just think that when women get together and chat, they should have a little treat. Life is busy and complicated, so why not enjoy the little things."

"Like guinea pigs?"

"Analena! You *are* a writer, so witty with words. Yes, enjoy the little things like adorable guinea pigs."

Once Piepie had our drinks made, we carried them over to the couch. "To the little things." We clanked our glasses and eased onto the couch. "I must know the history behind your name, as you're the first Piepie I've ever met."

She took a sip and set the glass on the coffee table. "First, it's spelled just as you would say it, pie-pie. And would you believe I don't even like pie?"

"What a bummer. I love a good pie. I mean, crust is basically bread, and it might be a crime not to love bread."

"You've got me there. I love bread."

I sprang up from the couch. "Janet dropped off a loaf of her delicious sourdough bread the other day, and I've been trying not to eat the entire thing. How does bread and cheese sound?"

"Sounds like we're going to become great friends." Piepie picked up her glass.

"And thank you, the chocolate martini is delicious."

"So glad you like it. Where were we? Oh yes, back to my name. It's not an actual name. What I mean is my Guyai—it's what I called my grandma because as a child I couldn't say *Granny*, she's from South Africa. You should hear her accent, it's beautiful. Anyway, she used to always call me her little pumpkin, but the Afrikaans word was a bit too confusing. It was spelled P-A-M-P-O-E-N-T-J-I-E, so she shortened my nickname to Poenie Pie and then shortened it again because everyone loves to make things shorter, and that became Piepie."

"This is so fascinating. My name has no history or story behind it. I'm born, and like a sticker on a rump roast, they slapped me with Analena McCoy." I sipped the martini. "So legally you're not Piepie?"

She chuckled. "Legally, Piepie is my name now. I mean, not everyone likes their name, and after all, it is your identity, so why not make it what you want." She leaned back on the couch. "Enough about me, what about you? Are you close to your parents?"

I swallowed. "They passed a while back, but we weren't too close. It wasn't your typical parent-child relationship."

Piepie and I spent the next hour sharing stories of life and love, but she wouldn't budge on what Todd's two-pronged plan was. By the time she headed back to her condo, the chocolate martini had gone to my head, and I was useless for doing any more writing for the day. I curled up on the couch with a book from the community library and removed the bird feather I was using as a bookmark. The book wasn't a new release, but it wasn't from the Jane Austen era like my typical reads. While I found the story intriguing, I couldn't let Amy know, or I'd never hear the end of another one of her famous I Told You So speeches.

Chapter 11

The thing about holidays was not the holiday itself, it was how horrible I was at remembering their exact dates. And not having work meant no schedule and thus no idea what day of the month it was. Plus, working in the grocery store, we knew when Valentine's Day, St. Patrick's, Easter, Halloween, Thanksgiving, Christmas, and even New Year's Eve was, even if we didn't have giant displays announcing it or the day off. It came down to the customers. They were busier, snappier, and short-tempered. I've witnessed people fighting over the last turkey and the last bag of Christmas tree-shaped chocolates. And it was as funny and ruthless as they portray it on TV, especially if the store manager is as tall as a fifth grader and doesn't do well with confrontation.

I'd been posting daily social media snapshots of my typewriter desk view and the stack of pages for my manuscript getting higher. And thanks to being someplace that actually had four seasons, I was able to post all the fall colors from the maple trees around the condo.

Halloween had passed, although I didn't hand out candy because I couldn't control myself with it being in the condo. I didn't want fun size to inevitably turn into my bigger bum size. The question for this year was where Thanksgiving fell on the calendar. Some years, that turkey really tried to squeeze its hefty body into December. To be fair, I've been knee-deep in my first draft. No author really tells you how hard it is to write a book. While they post and say they spent time writing, they don't tell you about the many hours, even days they spent staring into space. Deleting pages, or in my case, ripping out paper and starting all over again. Turns out I don't need the internet to distract me, my mind did a fine job on its own.

I needed a break from writing and took a short drive to the library that was sandwiched between Ocean Cove and Crooked River. I loved that they had gone all out with their Thanksgiving decorations. Fall leaves and acorns of all sizes were stuck to the sides of bookcases or resting on top. I'd visited a few times since moving here so that I could check out books on police procedures for my story, then sat in a chair overlooking a park with a small tree-lined lake. Something about the trees in all their golden shades of orange put me in a trance nearing a medicated state. It was unlike anything I'd seen in Nevada and made me want to change the location of my story simply to write a paragraph on the beauty I saw. While there were benches around the lake, the library sat on a knoll, allowing for a view that appeared much like the planetarium's open sky. My second favorite reason for coming to the library was the familiarity it brought, as though I'd been coming here since I was a child. The staff were nice, but it was more than that. Every time I walked through the front doors, it felt like a warm-from-the-dryer sweater wrapping itself around me, stopping me from shivering from the cold.

Although Todd had made me a desk, I enjoyed the atmosphere of the library. I would take breaks from writing a few times a week and bring my typed pages to hand edit with my favorite purple pen that made my notes look less harsh. I refused to use red; it was simply too angry. When I marked up my manuscript with purple, it seemed kinder. Then once I got home, I'd retype the pages to produce a fresh draft to work with on the first round of upcoming edits.

Even though I didn't technically live in Ocean Cove, the library had a nonresident program, which allowed me to check out books and my new favorite activity, old movies and TV shows. The library had become my Blockbuster. Which came in handy since the Wi-Fi seemed to go out every few weeks. The rental condo may not have had a desk, but I'd found a DVD player in the hall closet and, thanks to YouTube, figured out how to connect it to the TV.

"Fancy seeing you here." I recognized the voice and turned away from the window that overlooked the small tree-lined park.

"Janet? Hi." She had a canvas bag slung over her shoulder. The turkey brooch on her sweater gleamed in the library's overhead lights.

"This doesn't look like research." Janet tilted her head at the window. "I hope your writing is going well?"

"It's going." I waved the stack of typed paper and purple-penned notes in her direction. "I like to come here and enjoy the view while I edit. Change of scenery. What brings you by? I thought the condo's library had plenty of books to pick from?"

"Oh, I don't dare touch those." Janet's face was serious, and her vision darted around us. "The books are haunted," she whispered.

I think about the two books I borrowed from there sitting back on the coffee table at the condo. "Haunted how?"

"I've seen them move . . . the books . . . from the shelf."
Janet wrapped her hand around the top strap of her purse.
"Maybe you could write about that, add it to your story."

"The way my story is going, I could add a ghost and
elephant in, and it wouldn't throw off the storyline." I
laughed.

"Check with Todd. I think he's seen the most activity.
Talking about ghosts gives me the heebie-jeebies." Janet
loosened her pearl-white scarf. "What are your plans for
Thanksgiving?"

"Plans? None. I'm not sure what I'll do." I set the stack
of edited pages onto my backpack in the chair next to me.

"That's not acceptable, it's Thanksgiving."

"I haven't really been big on celebrating holidays since
my divorce, well to be fair, since the last few years before
my divorce. Usually, back home I worked any available
overtime or went to my best friend's house and crashed her
family time. Besides, this Thanksgiving, I need to work on
my manuscript. I'm falling behind."

Janet shrugged her shoulders. "Well, you know where
I live if you change your mind. Of course, Yo-Yo will be
there. I hope you figure something out; it's no fun to spend
the holidays alone." She spun on her heel and headed toward the circulation desk.

Writing really was becoming a great excuse to get out
of doing anything that scared me, worried me, gave me
anxiety, or caused me to think about the past. Leaning
back in the fabric chair, I crossed my arms and gazed out
the window. I could use this manuscript as my crutch for
anything. Time to do laundry? Nope, I had a novel to work
on. Make a salad? Nope, that takes too much time away
from my manuscript. Work out and lose weight? Nope,
that darn story.

I peeked down at my thighs. That diet was going as well as my manuscript. They still needed a lot of work.

I sighed and leaned back in the chair, wrapping my jacket closer around my chest. What had Janet meant about the books being haunted at the community building? Could books even be haunted? And if they could, why were they? The real question was, was I willing to ask Todd about it?

Thanksgiving. I envisioned the last one I celebrated. It was with Dawson. We ordered a pre-cooked Thanksgiving box meal. Even though I wanted to make a turkey and all the fixings with him as a couple's activity, he vetoed it faster than I could finish asking. That was our last fall holiday together. That New Year's Eve, I told him I wanted to call it quits. Talk about fireworks at midnight. And since then, I just hadn't been in the mood to celebrate Thanksgiving at all.

Maybe this year I could make a turkey—a little one, half a breast, some stuffing, mashed potatoes, gravy, and sweet potato pie. All from scratch. My novel's main character was a retired chef; it could be book research. I needed to keep the baking to a minimum with my budget—nothing overboard—but a simple Thanksgiving might be nice. A way for me to cover up the thoughts of the many pre-cooked ones with Dawson. I was starting fresh after all, and what better way than with a fresh bird?

Flipping the page in my notebook, I wrote a list of items I'd need from the grocery store. The author-induced loneliness was growing on me, and I was eager to continue to venture down this path of unknown outcomes for both the novel and myself.

Chapter 12

I was reaching into the oven to pull out my very juicy, slightly golden-brown turkey when I heard a male voice outside frantically yell, "Dylan!"

Setting the glass dish on the trivet, I ran to the door, flinging it open with the oven mitts still on my hands.

Todd came flying past. "Dylan!"

Who is Dylan?

"Todd, what's going on?" I called out, taking off in a jog after him, but noticed the dog was right next to him. "Who is Dylan?"

I kept my distance. The massive black-and-tan dog was not paying attention to me, but I was paying very close attention to him. He wasn't on a leash.

"He's gone. I don't know, I was just showering, and I got out and he wasn't on the couch anymore." Todd shoved his hands through his wet hair. "His mother was right. I can't take care of him."

"Who's Dylan?" I kept the mitts on my hands because it was cold, and the wind was blowing and smacking the rain like little shards of glass against my face.

"My son. He has autism."

Son?

That's when I looked at Todd and noticed he was bare-foot, in jeans and only a long-sleeved green shirt. His face displayed terror, fear, and loss.

"You need shoes and a jacket," I said.

"So do you."

I looked down and noticed I was in socks, which were now wet and dirty. "Crap. Okay, well, we're here now. Can your dog do anything?"

Todd's eyes widened. "Why didn't I think of that?" He kneeled to the dog's level. "Go find Dylan."

The dog didn't move but tilted its head.

"Find Dylan. Go get Dylan."

With that, the dog took off, sniffing around the parking lot, heading back toward the condos. The dog ran with long strides of grace, and I found myself staring at it.

"Where do you think Dylan could have gone?"

"Maybe the playground." Todd followed directly behind the dog.

I stayed several steps back in case the dog turned and headed my way. "You go that way; I'll check around on the other side of the building, in case he went looking for seashells or rocks. We'll find him. I've never lost a kid in my grocery store."

The right side of his lip twitched, then he jogged toward the playground area, the direction his dog was heading. I hurried towards the other edge of the condos and looped around the backside. Although I'm rusty, I prayed, unsure if I was doing it correctly since it had been years.

I squinted through the rain, which was coming down harder now than a few minutes before, making it challenging to see. But my mind went to Todd and the fact that he had a son. A son who had autism. He'd never mentioned it, and I'd never seen him with a child coming or going from his condo. And it seemed like something that might come up, but as a childless adult, what did I know?

Exiting the grassy mounds, I reached the sand, no longer able to see the difference between the rain-soaked sand and the ocean-washed sand. The scent and taste of sea salt were strong in the air. I glanced to the left and the right, hoping to spot a boy. Part of me felt that if I was the one to find him, I'd feel as though I'd finally made some sort of difference to someone's life. The last several months of author isolation were wearing on me. I didn't realize how much being a grocery store cashier had provided purpose in my life. After all, food was one of the three staples of life. Luckily, I worked for a small chain that had yet to install self-checkouts. I also knew that when it did happen, our staffing would be cut, and I hoped that my fifteen-some years was enough to keep me on the payroll.

There was not a single soul on the beach, and after another double check, I headed back towards the playground. My hand smacked my chest when I spotted Todd and a little boy coming towards the parking lot.

I jogged up to them, stopping short when I realized the dog was with them. "Thank goodness!"

"He was hiding in the tube that connects the slides. Whidbey sniffed him out and barked at me until I was standing in front of the tube." Todd held Dylan's hand. The boy laughed to himself and flicked his fingers back and forth, holding them close to his eyes.

"I'm glad he's okay." I kept my distance and made eye contact with Whidbey's amber golden eyes for a few seconds.

Todd glanced down at the dog and gave some strokes to its head. "Sorry if we interrupted your Thanksgiving."

"Not at all. I was just making a few things, busy with the book and all." I wrapped my arms around myself as the adrenaline subsided, allowing me to feel the weather again.

Todd made his way under the cover of the second-story landing, while I followed with at least an SUV distance between us. Dylan squealed and jumped as they walked, completely unaware that he'd nearly given his father a heart attack.

"How come you never mentioned you had a son?" I blurted, standing near my front door.

"It's complicated. People either feel sorry for me or ignore me once they find out. I split custody with his mom, and when he's with me, life pretty much stops any regular activities, which often includes work. He's in a day program, but his meltdowns can be pretty severe, and I often have to leave work to go get him when I have him for the week."

I shivered but tried not to let Todd see. I wanted our conversations to continue without him thinking I was going to run the other way or pity him like everyone else. "So, is that why I haven't seen you around much?"

"Yes, his mom had to travel for work, and I had him longer than normal. I've been trying to keep him as busy as possible. He loves to go to the aquarium; we have season passes. It's the only place he doesn't throw tantrums. But with it being Thanksgiving, they are closed."

"That's great that you've found something that works for him."

Todd grabbed hold of Whidbey's collar. "Oh, don't think you're getting away from this fear of animal thing. I'm just preoccupied at the moment." He glanced down at the dog. "If things are burned, you can always join us. We're going out for dinner. I'm not a fan of cooking such a big Thanksgiving feast for myself. Dylan refuses to eat turkey or mashed potatoes . . . or anything mashed, green, or pumpkin related. And the place we go to serves chicken nuggets and fries, his favorite. He eats only about five foods, so I take what I can get."

I raised my shoulders. "That must be challenging." I wanted to kneel and make eye contact with Dylan to say hi, but his eyes were focused everywhere else, and Whidbey was right next to him. "Happy Thanksgiving, Todd."

Todd smiled. "Happy Thanksgiving." He turned and began heading up the stairs, Whidbey on his right and Dylan on his left, putting his feet together on the steps, slowing them down. "We're leaving at five if you decide you want to join us. And don't forget you still need to help me go Christmas shopping for my sister and mom."

"Thanks, and I haven't forgotten," I said, and gave a wave although he didn't turn around to see.

I headed inside my condo, acutely aware that I'd sort of pushed everyone in the condo complex away, making excuses to isolate myself over the last month. I'd gained five pounds instead of losing five in the last few months. Taking a deep breath, I let it out and closed my eyes, then they popped open. Something was burning. I rushed to the stove and lifted the lid. The water had boiled dry, and the one lone potato was burned and wrinkly at the bottom.

I glanced at the clock on the stove, then at the front door, then at the burned potato. No, this was Todd's time with his son. And I knew nothing about being around an autistic child. Were there rules? Things I could or couldn't do that would cause a tantrum? And other than eating what I hoped would be a somewhat tasty dinner, minus the mashed potatoes, I had to figure out the hole in my plot.

I put the lid back on the pot and straightened my posture, raising my chin into the air. This was my Thanksgiving, and I wouldn't let some burned potato set me back. Besides, I could always use this food incident as inspiration for my novel.

"Nothing is lost to a writer!" I held up the wooden spoon. "Now, where'd I put the wine bottle opener?"

Chapter 13

I watched as the clouds created a misty haze outside the slider while I was hopelessly trapped in the writing phase known by authors as butt-in-chair. I'd been sitting there long enough to know that if I stood up my bottom would be checkered with the patio chair's pattern.

Behind me were twenty-six discarded, balled-up pages that I'd ripped from the typewriter and tossed over my shoulder. I'd just pulled the story through the preclimax and into the climax only to have no clue how to transition into the falling action and resolution of my novel. How had I made it this far only to come up short? I needed to satisfy the reader and frankly, myself. I wanted a great ending just as much as the reader.

My wrists cramped and my spine throbbed. I glanced at the couch, longing to be sitting on it with a laptop. What a far better and more relaxing way to write a book than this 1940s relic.

"What was I thinking?" I brought my hands to my face and cupped my cheeks, pushing them back towards my ears. "This sucks."

Self-doubt welled up in me, turning into a low boil rage. So many authors made writing a book look easy. They conned us into thinking it was a simple task full of coffee mugs, soft pajamas, and snacks. Where were the authors that told the truth about how hard it was to create something out of nothing? To analyze a paragraph so many times that I'd memorized it and didn't want to read it ever again? They were too busy showing colorful checkmarks on their pretty graphs of the two-thousand words a day they wrote.

"I'm over here acting like this stupid typewriter that keeps malfunctioning is going to produce all my author dreams."

I breathed deeply and closed my eyes. Day after day of isolation, focusing on a story was not just hard but emotionally draining. Like a solid black puzzle that you wanted to complete but had no idea how to even start it and when you did you had no idea how you'd finish it. I was stuck between wanting to give up and the need to keep going. My thoughts drifted to my life back in Nevada and how excited I'd been to come here, the fantasy of it all. And I couldn't allow that dream to die because I was in a bad mood and something on my typewriter broke every week.

"Put on your big girl pants."

I sat up straight and threaded a new piece of paper into the typewriter, but when I began to type, the machine jammed, again. This time it was the T key. It wasn't leaving the ink on the page. I tapped the T key hard, then harder, then I started to rapid fire all my pent-up frustration through my pointer finger out on that T. I was breathing heavily by the time I'd settled down, yet the T had decided it was done being useful.

"I don't need that letter anyways, I can make do with the rest. Any first draft is far from perfect." I brought my posture back up and continued to type without a working T when the shift key stopped working as well. That, I needed.

"Are you freaking kidding me? I have ten chapters to go. Ten!"

The rage I hadn't done a good job of shoving to the side came roaring back. I picked up the typewriter and flung the slider open with my pinky and ring finger. I stepped up to the flimsy railing.

"You worthless piece of crap!" I chucked that typewriter like a discus at a track meet and watched it sail over the railing, over the grassy strip, and land with a thump on the sand.

"Damn." I rubbed the top part of my right shoulder where it was hurting.

"What the actual heck?" Todd appeared to my left.

"Hey," I said and leaned forward on the railing.

"No, not hey. That's not what you say to someone that you nearly take out with a flying typewriter."

"Sorry. And it wasn't flying. It was sailing peacefully to its new home."

Todd glanced at me and back at the typewriter wedged into the sand. "No, last I checked the typewriter belongs inside. Why are you throwing a fifteen-pound anything off your patio?"

"I have no use for it anymore."

"Is this a short-people thing? Throwing heavy objects without looking?"

"You're tall enough, shouldn't you have seen it coming?" I stood up straight.

"I'm not usually on the lookout for flying—sorry, sailing—typewriters." Todd rested his hands on his hips. "Seriously, Analena, what's going on?"

I huffed and exhaled a sigh loud enough to be heard over the crashing ocean waves ramping up for a storm.

"I just can't anymore. The stupid typewriter is constantly breaking, and my story is already broken."

Todd walked a few feet to the edge of my railing and rested his hand on it. "Your story is not broken; your typewriter might be. But you don't need the typewriter, you never did. The typewriter doesn't make you an author." He took the side of my head into his hand, and I gently shut my eyes at the comfort of his touch. "All you need—and ever needed—is right in that brilliant head of yours. It doesn't matter if you write on paper or on a laptop. Only you can write your story. It might take you five drafts, it might take you fifty, but only you can tell the story you want to tell because it's all about your talent, not the machine you use to get the words out there."

Can you please never take your hand off me? "Thanks for the pep talk. I'm just drained; like I have nothing left to give this story. I didn't understand the depths of writing. It's not as though I'm writing a memoir. It's a thriller for goodness' sake."

Todd's hand drifted away from my head as though it was a boat going back out to sea. "Writing is a challenge. But it's nothing that you can't accomplish."

I gave him a weak smile. Todd turned and made his way out to the typewriter, hoisting it out of the sand. He shook it left and right as sand fell from it. "Sorry about that, fella." He squeezed it to his chest.

"Are you hugging an object?"

"He had feelings about being thrown out like an ex's bag of clothes."

I shook my head. "And why do you assume it's a he?"

"Because it's manly." Todd held it up. "See this, paper support, like a man's support."

I pointed at it. "What about those two pattern knobs?"

Todd was clearly blushing as he averted his eyes from mine. "So, you want this back or not?"

"Fine. It can't be any more broken than it was before."

He set it on the railing, and our fingertips touched in the exchange. "I think it can be. Sand is never good wedged into anything."

"Hey, where is Whidbey?" I kept the typewriter resting on the railing.

"He escaped."

"What?" My hands let go of the typewriter as it wobbled.

Todd reached for it before it toppled backwards. "I'm not saving this twice."

My heart was racing. "What do you mean lost? Can he jump over these railings?" My vision darted all around the exposed patio.

"I'm joking. He's a German shepherd, they don't get lost. He's up in the condo. I came back down because I ran out of poop bags. He decided he had to go three times, and I only brought two with me." Todd pointed out at the sky. "I thought it was about to start raining and didn't really want to deal with a wet dog, so I took him home, and then came back down to go pick up the poopies."

I pressed my lips together, muffling a laugh. *Poopies.* Why did it sound adorable when Todd said *poopies*?

"What's funny?"

"On nothing. Thank you again, Todd. For rescuing my typewriter."

"It better be worth it. I went through a lot to get that back for you." He grinned. "I expect you to finish that first draft. Otherwise, it was all for nothing."

I breathed through my nose and nodded. "Yes, it better be worth it."

Chapter 14

"No, no, no!" I cried out.

"It's true!" Todd laughed. "As much as I don't want to admit it."

"You're lying." I smacked his arm. "Ghost aren't real."

We're sitting on a very small couch in front of the fireplace at the community building, both in workout clothes. Light danced behind the glass and illuminated the bookcases over our shoulders. There was a minimally decorated Christmas tree that one resident dragged out of the closet that sat next to the fireplace. Its age was showing as there were bare spots from missing branches, and the whole thing needed a bit of fluffing to look less like the narrow shape of a box. I was glad Mason was not working out at the gym. Every time we ran into each other, all he did was glare at me as though I've done something wrong, even though I know I didn't.

Todd glanced over at the bookcase. "I saw a book hovering and then I let out this unmanly scream and it fell to the floor as though I'd startled someone, causing them to drop it." He motioned with his hands outward as though a magician showing he has nothing to hide. "Didn't I see you borrowing some books from here?"

"Yes, why?"

"Nothing odd happened?"

"Odd, like they opened on their own?" I scrunched up my face and raised an eyebrow. "No, of course not. Books moving on their own? That's not even believable. And trust me, I've done my fair share of research on what is believable when it comes to mysteries."

"Sure, sure, it's just a different world for you down there." Todd pointed at the ground.

"I'm not that short."

"You're right, but you found awesome Christmas presents for my mom and sister that I would have missed."

"You did not have me help you go gift shopping because you're too lazy to bend down and check lower shelves!"

"Hey, don't question my level of laziness."

I didn't respond and stared at him, observing his facial features, memorizing them for some unknown reason.

"Analena?"

I shook my head. "I enjoyed helping you shop, but I don't think it was a fair trade for the desk."

"You're right. That's why I'll need your help again in April to shop for my sister's birthday present."

"I'm game. As long as you still want to hang out with me in four months."

Todd grinned. "I'll still want to hang out with you in four years."

I swallowed, and took a deep breath, hoping it would keep the rouge from giving away my feelings about his comment.

"Outside of shopping with me, is there a reason why I haven't seen you much?" Todd asked, but he didn't make eye contact. "Basically, at all lately?"

"Not that I can think of. I've been working on the manuscript. I'm more than halfway done with the first draft."

"It's just," he paused. "You've become a hermit."

He was right. Most days I was still in my pajamas at one in the afternoon. "I didn't mean to hide from everyone. But so many of you have pets, I mean whenever I leave the condo it's like a zoo out here." I leaned my head back onto the couch and stared up at the ceiling. "And Piepie mentioned a two-prong plan that I must admit, has kept me behind closed doors too."

"Ahh yes, the plan. It's a slow plan. You can thank work and Dylan for putting that on hold." He raised his index finger in the air. "But rest assured, it's back in play."

My head popped up. "I won't be resting anything."

Todd chuckled, and if it weren't for the Christmas tree, I wouldn't have noticed how much it sounded like Santa's laugh from all those childhood movies. "So, the typewriter—is it still typing and the desk working okay?"

"The desk is great, thank you. The typewriter has made a semi-recovery, not better, but not worse. From time to time I find grains of sand on the desk. I still don't have an office chair, though, so I've stacked a few pillows to make the patio chair work. Plus, I get up and walk around every thirty minutes to prevent chair butt."

Todd's mouth turned up on the right. "Chair butt?"

"I have this theory that you can get a flat bottom from sitting too long. You know, the antithesis of callipygian."

"Well, then you must get up a lot because your bottom is not flat."

My face flushed instantly as though I'd just downed an entire glass of wine. "As long as it's not a badonkadonk."

"You've been listening to Trace Adkins a little too much."

"You can never listen to too much classic country music."

Todd shook his head. "Just don't hide out too much from living life. There was this one author, I used to love his books. I couldn't wait for the next one to come out. But over the years, with each new release, they grew dark and one-dimensional. I know they say writers need to get focused and into the writing zone, but you need to make sure life doesn't pass you by. One of my favorite authors was going through some things on a personal level, but instead of taking the time to focus on life, he pushed through his writing and published subpar books. It was pretty disappointing."

"Well, I can't afford any hiccups when I must watch my time and money. It's not easy to go out and gallivant around," I whined.

"You do you; I'm only calling it like I see it. Besides, I made you a desk, so I guess I'm your accomplice in this endeavor." He rested his arm on the back of the couch. "I get that life has its challenges. My wife and I divorced because Dylan has autism. We fought a lot. We couldn't seem to find common ground on how to raise him. What services to try to get him. When he was an infant, we noticed a few things, but as new parents, we didn't know up from down, and it wasn't like we could fix him. She wanted to put him in ABA."

"A-B-what?"

"Applied behavioral analysis. They work with kids to help with their behaviors and increase their social interactions. I wanted him to take the normal school route. They even did an IEP for him."

I raised my hand. "I'm not familiar with all these acronyms."

"Sorry, an IEP is something the school does—a planning document. It's an individualized education plan to help a child who is scoring behind other students. It allows Dylan, or any kid with one, to get additional help with physical, occupational, and speech therapy and specialized transportation and a little personal care support in school."

"That must be an enormous benefit, I can see why you pushed for that."

"I thought so too. I wanted his life to be as normal as possible. I just didn't realize that it wouldn't work for Dylan. My ex did more research, talked to other parents, and really knew what was best for him. We were arguing more than we were talking. Kids affect marriages in many ways, but no one really talks about how much the effect is when your kid has a disability."

I set my hand on his arm. "I can't imagine."

"Your turn."

I turned back to the fireplace. I was a decent listener, and while I didn't mind sharing, it was different when I was talking to someone I was attracted to. "It's easier to hide from your failures than to face them. And I've never been good at facing things. In my marriage, I knew it was not going to work out, but instead of being upfront about it, I allowed it to drag on. As the years went on, I noticed there was hesitation in my voice when I told Dawson I loved him. He didn't notice it because it was just a beat, a simple, single pause. And now, with this manuscript, I'm losing the drive to sit down and write because my mind is busy trying to figure out other things on my plate. Negativity and self-doubt have found their way into the process, just like they did in my marriage. It's a much bigger undertaking than I ever imagined, but I don't want to quit. I can't quit. But I don't know what to do, and I've wedged myself into this crevice, where it's dark and uncomfortable."

"Does anything ever go as planned?"

"My divorce did."

Todd laughed, really laughed. It was so deep and hardy that I was swept into it with him and snickered. I didn't mean it to be funny, but it was true. And it was the only thing that I felt I did right. "Didn't you mention you'd divorced two times?"

"Yes, my second divorce. It was a quick marriage. I jumped into it after six months, unaware of how different we were. We drifted apart as quickly as we got together. My focus was on work, and her focus was on her law career. It ended amicably. Later, she actually invited me to her wedding. I went and had fun."

I pressed my lips together as I smiled. "My divorce was much different." I thought for a second. "Still is different. He can't seem to move on, while I have." I took a long drink from my water bottle. "Do you ever look back and wonder if you married the wrong woman?"

"Did you marry the wrong man?"

"Yes and no. Love is so powerful you can feel it. You're in it as though you're getting swept up by a tornado. But for some, it doesn't hold as firm. Like a tornado takes a piece of straw and shoves it into a tree trunk, while other times it can set a jar of pickles down undamaged half a town away. It's not the same for all of us. Some might not even get a chance to experience the tornado."

"I would even say, to some degree, there is love regarding my prior wives; I'm just not *in* love with them." Todd readjusted his hips on the couch.

"Does that make divorce not about falling out of love, but falling out of *being* in love? The love that makes two people's souls connect either by lightning or by a gravitational pull. Something that is so quick you don't see it coming or have time to react. Have you ever had that feeling when a person walks by you, and it's as though you're drawn to something you can't see but feel, like a ghost is sweeping through you?"

"Now you want to talk about ghosts." He eyed the bookcase.

I laughed. "Completely different ghosts. I'm being serious."

"That's a shame."

I leaned forward. "It's an emotion that overcomes my entire body, and it's full, heavy, yet light. Light enough that it keeps on going, but heavy enough that you can feel it pass through. It's like an enormous sigh that everything is perfectly falling together and into place."

Todd stood up, grabbing his water bottle off the floor. "Interesting."

"I've scared you away."

Todd shook his head. "No, I really need to grab Whidbey for his walk."

I nodded, not fully believing him.

"Now, about Christmas. Dylan's mom has him since I got him for Thanksgiving. So, how about we do something? No gifts or anything. Just get you out from behind your typewriter. We can watch a holiday movie, make something holiday-ish to eat."

I crossed my arms. "Hmm."

"I'll even make it pajama attire."

"Now you have a deal."

Todd headed for the door, and I noticed outside the window it had started to snow. Big, fat flakes drifted down from the cloudy sky.

I dashed to the window like an eight-year-old on Christmas morning running to her stocking on the mantel in seconds. "Oh my gosh. Snow." My index finger tapped the window. "That's snow!"

Todd eyed me, his eyebrows raised. "Are you okay?"

I grabbed him around both biceps, which would forever leave a lingering impression in my memory, shaking him. "I've never seen snow!"

Chapter 15

I nearly yanked Todd's arm from its socket trying to get us out of the community building's door. The sky above was muted pink, like watered-down cotton candy. It appeared to have just started falling as it was only beginning to stick to the tops of the cars and the grass. I lifted my hand, palm up, toward the sky, allowing for the snowflakes to land, but before I could inspect them, they melted. I couldn't help but twirl around, and when I focused back on Todd, he had this childlike grin on his face.

"What?" I asked.

"You . . . it's just, you're cute."

I waved his comment off, as he was missing the point. "It's snowing! How can you *not* be excited?"

"Try driving in it or putting on a roof before it starts coming down."

"Okay, well, but right now, neither of those things are happening." I lifted my hands up toward the sky. "Do you think it'll last? How much until it piles up? How much do we need to make a snow angel?" I tilted my head. "Snowman?"

Todd crossed his arms. He must have been cold in just shorts and a T-shirt. I looked down and realized I was only a little better dressed in yoga pants and a T-shirt.

"We need at least two inches to get us a snow angel, but we'll need more for a snowman, unless it's a miniature one."

I shrugged my shoulders. "I can do miniature." I patted my yoga pants, forgetting which of the six pockets I'd shoved my phone into. "Will the weather app tell us?"

Holding out my phone, the snowflakes landed on the screen, and Todd stood over my shoulder. I could feel his breath and smelled it too—sweet, like mango flavored gum.

I held my phone up to his level. "I don't know what I'm looking for?"

When he took it, our icy fingers brushed up against each other, and a shiver, not from the cold weather, rolled through my limbs.

"Looks like it will snow for at least a couple of hours. It's not super unusual to get a dusting, but we don't see the same accumulation like they get inland. If you really want to get a snowy experience, I can take you farther inland. But we'd bring Whidbey. He loves the snow."

Todd handed my phone back to me, and we walked toward the condos. "I think I'll wait it out here and see what becomes of this snow."

"Right. You're *pet*-rified." Todd took one step for every two of mine.

"I'm surprised you can find any jokes up there. Aren't you suffering from oxygen deprivation that high in the air?" I craned my neck up to him.

"I'm sorry I couldn't hear you all the way down there."

"Anyways, about the snow!" I shouted.

"This snow. You know it's different snow inland." He used his thumb to point behind him.

I leaned around him. "No, this snow is better. It's softer, prettier."

Todd chuckled. "Okay, but you'd be missing out on harder, uglier snow."

"That's not a selling point."

He was now directly in front of me. "How do you know? You're new to snow."

I was so delirious from him standing so close that snowflakes couldn't fall between us I'd lost all common sense. "You're right."

His lips twitched.

"Wait, no. I've seen enough snow-filled movies to know, the fluffier the better."

Then we just stood there, me looking up at him as snowflakes that shimmered like diamonds stuck to the lower strands of my hair. A car door slammed in the distance somewhere, but I didn't flinch.

"Thank goodness I got home just in time," Piepie's voice came from behind us. "What are you two doing standing out in the cold dressed like that?"

"I was leaving the gym," Todd said, turning around.

"I was heading to the gym." That was when I noticed Piepie was not alone.

At the end of a leash was her furry ash-black dog. It might have weighed the same as a bag of groceries, but to me it was huge. I grabbed hold of Todd's arm and used it to shield myself as I stepped behind him.

"You know Valentino's a twenty-pound dog, not a twenty-pound spider, right?" Todd stepped to the left, exposing me to the dog that was only getting closer to us.

"Should he be running around in the snow? Shouldn't you carry him or something?"

Piepie pulled up the leash a bit. "They haven't salted the pavement or anything."

My focus had gone from the snow, to Todd, and now to Valentino, the small but clearly related-to-a-black-bear dog.

I let go of Todd's arm and walked backwards. "I really need to get back to my writing."

"What about the snow?" Todd turned around.

"Like you said, needs to pile up more."

Todd stood between Piepie and me, just as Janet's condo door swung open.

"Hey, Yo-Yo, it's your best friend." Janet exited the door, with the Yorkie on a leash and small green Croc-like boots on its paws.

Valentino yanked on his leash when he spotted Yo-Yo and let out a bark. I jumped, startled. Yo-Yo's tail wagged and his paws pounced with what I assumed was excitement. If I headed towards my door, I was too close to Yo-Yo, but if I headed back toward Todd, I was too close to Valentino.

"You know, I need to get to the gym. I never got that workout in." I waved my water bottle in the air and scurried between them, noticing the pavement had become slippery from the sticking snow. My shoes were not gripping, and both my hands went out for balance.

"Don't run away from your fears," Todd called after me.

"Running burns calories!" I dashed towards the door and shoved the key into the lock.

I wiped my sneakers on the rug inside the door of the community building. Behind me, the snow was really coming down, and working out was the last thing I wanted to do, especially since there were no windows in the gym. I wanted to curl up on the couch, turn on my fireplace and watch it fall while I read a book and sipped wine. Being a responsible adult was overrated.

But if I convinced myself not to work out today, I would get into a habit of excuses, and I'd made enough already. Punching level one with a ten percent incline into the machine, I began walking, thinking back to how close Todd and I had gotten outside. And what we'd shared with each other on the community couch earlier, felt like a therapy session with a friend. I'd been speaking from experience earlier about the whole gravitational pull into perfection, because I'd felt it when I first met Todd. And it was only getting stronger every time we were together.

Chapter 16

My workout ran short, but I got a mile walk in. I simply couldn't lift weights knowing that snowflakes danced down from the clouds outside. After dropping off my water bottle and grabbing a very dated marshmallow-shaped jacket, because I didn't use it much in Nevada, I headed down to the beach.

Snow had spread across the sand in a random pattern as the ocean waves kept pulling it back towards them like little kids' hands collecting it to make a snowman. The nip in the air was not as bone-chilling as when it rained, which made for a more relaxing walk.

As the snow painted the edges of every tree and balcony overhang, I couldn't help staring as though it were a museum painting. I'd seen nothing like it before and couldn't wrap my head around how there was no one else out enjoying the magical display. If this happened in my neighborhood back home, everyone would be outside with their mouths agape and a bucket to capture it and save it in their freezers.

My phone pinged in my pocket, and I pulled it out. Then I grumbled when I saw who it was from.

Dawson: Any plans for Christmas?

> Analena: No plans.

> Dawson: I'm doing something differ-
> ent this year.

> Analena: Good for you. I hope it turns
> out fun.

> Dawson: I think it will. So, you're just
> staying home?

> Analena: Yeah.

I reread the texts. Usually, he had more to say than just a few words back and forth. Maybe I was being too mean on my end. After all, we can still be friends, no need to act snotty.

> Analena: I really hope so. You de-
> serve to have a nice holiday. Say hi to
> your parents for me.

I wasn't sure why I said *deserve*. I didn't really feel that way. I guess in a way we all deserve good things, although looking back, our holidays were never a big to-do with my parents gone, and his family functions were awkward. We were the ones without the grandkids for them to spoil, which made it hard fit in during gatherings.

> **Dawson:** This Christmas will be different, just you wait.

> **Analena:** I sure hope so.

After I hit Send, I regretted my words. It sounded like I wasn't having a good time. So far, it was not going as planned, but I didn't want Dawson to think that. It was going well, so why had I responded that way? The last thing I wanted was for him to feel sorry for me, as though I'd made a mistake about this entire adventure. It was just like me to make a mess out of nothing.

If I stayed out too long, I feared I might lose my fingers to frostbite. I shook my head and shoved my hands deep into the jacket pockets. My fingertips touched something fuzzy in the depths of my jacket pockets.

"Oh!" I grabbed hold and yanked my hands back out, revealing fluffy purple mittens in each hand.

As I slid the mittens onto my hand, my phone rang, and spotting Amy's name on the screen I attempted to swipe it up but instead tossed my phone into the air. The mittens were clearly pre-cell phone, as they didn't have the fingertips that allowed for swiping. I picked my cell up off the snowy sand, brushing it off.

I set the phone on speaker. "Hey, one second," I told Amy. "You called at just the right time."

"Why is that?"

"It's snowing. Here, let me take a picture." I held the phone up, snapped a picture and then a selfie and sent them to her. After I got off the phone, I'd upload one to my social media.

"Wow, that's amazing. It looks like a Thomas Kinkade painting. I'm so jealous."

"You should be." I laughed. "Amy, it's life-changing. I know, I know, it's just snow, but there is a silence that I've never heard before. And the picture doesn't capture the reflective properties of how beautiful white can be. It's nothing like the white walls of my rental condo."

"I wish I was there to see it."

"Head up to Reno, they get snow there."

"A seven-hour drive with two girls fighting in the back seat the entire time? No thank you."

I continued my walk north on the beach, feeling caught between two different worlds, one of winter from the sky and one of summer from the ocean waves.

"We haven't talked in a month," I said, breaking the silence.

"It's been a month? Wow time really flies. What's up, I can tell something in your voice."

"Do you think it's weird that I don't like animals. You know, pets?"

"Yes."

"You could've at least put a few seconds of thought into it."

"Sorry, but your fear is over-the-top nonsensical. You couldn't even go to the zoo on our middle-grade school field trip. You always claimed they'd break out of their enclosures."

"I was protesting the caging of animals. Besides, zoo field trips are for elementary school kids."

Amy laughed. "That might have been a secondary reason, but not the first reason. Why do you care about this now?"

"No reason. It's just a zoo around here."

"Oh, does Measuring Tape Man have a pet?"

"The question is who doesn't have a pet."

"So, he does. Let me guess from how you described him he has a Lab, one of those chocolate ones."

"No, it's more like a wolf. It's an Arctic wolflike thing and it's got black-and-tan fur. Looks like a cop dog. He told me what kind it was, but I can't recall. Seems like it's five feet tall."

"Oh, it's a German shepherd. And they're not five feet tall." Amy covered the phone and yelled something in the distance. "Those girls, it's always something to fight about. Anyway, how is the writing going?"

"It's . . . going. I have good and bad days. Sometimes, writing a page takes me all day, and other times I can knock out ten pages. I don't know how writers who work full time find the time to create these worlds."

"When do I get to read it?"

"I don't know how I feel about sharing it until it's more polished. Once I get the first draft done, I'll be typing it onto a computer. The library has a pretty nice setup if my tablet doesn't work."

"You need me to read it. It's called a beta reader, and authors use them all the time, or so I've heard."

"I know, even so, don't hold your breath for a while." A large snowflake landed on the top of my eyelashes and obscured my vision. "Speaking of reading, have you read anything by Katherine Center?"

"She's only my favorite. But why are you asking? Is she in town? Hiding out? Like a secret writer's conference?"

"No." I bit my lip. "I started to read one."

"No way. You. Read. Current. Books? Are you sniffing the sea salt?"

I laughed. "No, there are a vast number of used books, like a little library in the community room, and I grabbed a few. I figured, why not?"

"Well, Hell must be serving ice cream."

"Fine, make fun of me all you want. I guess we won't be discussing it."

"That's not fair. Crap, I've gotta go. Jessica is crying. Enjoy your kid-free life."

We said goodbye, and I removed my mitten to end the call and slid the phone back into my pocket. Looking down at the snow meeting the sandy waves, it really did feel like it was mirroring my life, these two worlds melting into each other. One where I was a divorced woman going through all the things midlife threw at me, and the other where I was an author, living my dream with an ocean view. The two couldn't be more different and yet the same. After all, snow turned into water.

Chapter 17

I'd hoped the snow would somehow inspire the ending of my story to come flying out of my fingers as I typed, but it only distracted me from writing. So much for setting it in the summer when the dead of winter was happening outside. But at least it had given me something to look at when I stared blankly out the living room slider, resting my fingers on the typewriter keys.

The once-in-a-lifetime snow event affecting Ocean Cove meant the big, fluffy white flakes fell on and off for three days, and I'd not grown tired of it, but it sure made focusing much more difficult, which I didn't need. My goal in remaining on track was to have the first draft finished before the new year.

However, the snow melted quickly with the rain that came on Christmas Eve morning. Which made for a bit of everything feeling un-Christmasy. Residents had decorated the outside of their condos, but inside my rental condo didn't show a single sign of holiday cheer. It had slipped my mind to pack any Christmas decoration, and with my budget, I didn't know if stopping by the Dollar Store would be a smart decision.

There was a knock at my front door that brought me out of my thoughts. While it was one in the afternoon, it was Christmas Eve. Therefore, it was acceptable to open the door with my pajamas still on.

"Merry Christmas Eve!" Standing in front of me was Piepie and of course her hand was behind her back.

"Hi, Piepie." I scurried behind the door, afraid of her revealing one of her furry rodents as she struck up a conversation.

"I heard from Janet that you didn't have one bit of Christmas in that condo."

"Slight oversight when I was packing what I'd need for a year." I winced a smile.

"And that is why you need this!" Piepie swung her hand around, and I leaned back as though a hot potato was coming at me.

Instead, she presented me with a foot-tall tree in a red-Santa-cellophane-wrapped base. "And it smells like a Douglas fir! Don't worry, it's not a Doulgas *fur*."

I tilted my head. "Great play on words." I took it in my hands. "Piepie, that is so sweet of you. You really didn't have to."

Her face went serious. "Of course I did. You can't allow Christmas to pass by without a single display of joy. Now, I didn't get you any miniature ornaments. I wasn't sure of your style. Besides, it's so cute you don't have to decorate it."

"It's beautiful, thank you so much."

"Well, off to an early Christmas Eve dinner. I made pumpkin cake!"

"Sounds really yummy. Oh, because you don't do pie." I nodded.

"I should have made an extra one for you." Piepie frowned. "Now I feel bad."

"Don't, I don't need any more excuses to eat sweets."

She pouted and glanced at her watch. "We're late to my parents' house. But then again, Frank and I are always late to their place, so it's not like they'll be shocked. It's hard to be on time when you have to prepare your dogs for the drive—they get carsick—while securing the rest of their siblings at home." She heaved a sigh. "Have a very Merry Christmas, Analena."

"Thank you, Piepie, Merry Christmas, and drive safe."

She waved, and I shut the door, taking the tree over to the coffee table and setting it down. It really was an adorable little thing, nothing like a Charlie Brown tree. I stared at it for a bit, noticing it really needed a pop of something on it.

"Ahh!" I smiled and located a few sheets of blank paper and made my way to the kitchen for a pair of scissors.

I lowered onto the carpet and set my supplies on the coffee table. Then I turned on a Christmas movie, one of many that aired nonstop on a romance channel, and began cutting out mini snowflakes as I sipped on a glass of pinot gris. It was Christmas Eve after all.

The first few snowflakes fell apart when I opened them. It'd been ages since I last did the craft, and my memory failed me.

My phone rang, and just as I swiped it to answer, I realized it wasn't my best friend.

Dawson

I punched the green icon but didn't say anything.

"Merry Christmas, Analena."

I sighed. "Merry Christmas, Dawson."

"I just wanted to call and make sure you were . . . having a nice Christmas Eve day."

"Yes, and you?" Placing the last of the paper snowflakes on my tiny tree, I took a piney deep breath.

I looked around, and the little tree was small but mighty. Piepie was right, it was better than nothing.

"I decided to push the envelope this year," Dawson said.

"What? No *Die Hard*, a 6-pack of expensive beer, steak and potatoes with enough bacon crumbles on top to cause a trip to the emergency room for heart palpitations?"

"Not this year. What are you doing? *Home Alone* and cheese pizza?"

I sighed. "Maybe." The truth was I'd planned on streaming it. And I'd been in Ocean Cove long enough to feel ashamed I'd yet to try the local pizza place, which wouldn't be open tonight. I'd have to come up with a plan B. "You know that's what makes this Christmas special, just like last year, you don't have to deal with me."

"I want to deal with you."

There was a knock at the door, and I took the phone with me to answer it. Dawson was silent on the line. I swung open the door and gasped.

I gasped as though there was a dead body standing upright on the other side. I gasped as though Santa and his elves were standing there.

"Surprise, Analena!"

My hand found the door frame so I could regain my balance as my head spun. "Dawson?"

"Merry Christmas." He wrapped me up in a hug while my hands hung down next to my side. "Can I come in? Of course I can, it's Christmas Eve."

Dawson entered the condo, and I remained staring outside as though looking for the spaceship that brought him here.

He was dressed in jeans and a sweater as he flopped down on the couch, his big boots nearly knocking over my wineglass. "I figured we could whip up a little Christmas Eve dinner, light some candles, watch a movie. And maybe." He winked.

I fiercely shook my head. "How did you even find me? I never gave you my address."

"I have my ways." He picked up a snowflake.

I growled under my breath. Amy's husband. He and Dawson had been friends for years. He probably had him do the dirty work without Amy even knowing.

"Well, I have plans." Technically, they were for Christmas Day, but he didn't need to know that.

Dawson stood up and made his way over to me, taking both my hands in his. "I've been thinking, and I'm willing to change. I'll pick up my socks. I promise." He did the Scout's honor salute.

"It's not about the socks." I yanked my hands from his grasp.

"Then why is it all you talk about?"

"It's not *only* about the socks."

Now that I was standing, the wine seemed to have bounced to my toes and then back up to my head. Gosh, why had I not eaten something?

"Come on, An, Christmas is the season of giving, and I'm giving myself back to you."

"I think I threw up in my mouth."

"Don't be so dramatic." Dawson lifted the wineglass, gave it a sniff, and then a gulp.

"It's not about being easy, buddy. It's about the fact that . . . that." I flung hands out. "It's about you and me, but not together. You never supported me. You were never there for me. It was always something, but I saw how you treated your friends. I was always last. *We* were always last. We just didn't work."

"I don't understand. We worked just fine."

My hands acted as though they were snakes, flinging and flitting around. "Correct, you don't understand. You never did. I've done nothing with my life. I feel ugly and useless and horrible. Look at me, look at this." I grabbed at my stomach, taking the fat around my waist and squeezing it through my shirt.

"Yes, I see you. I'm looking." Dawson stared at my stomach.I ripped off my shirt and scrunched down my Capri jeans, allowing them to drop at my

feet. "No one wants this. I don't want this! And you never seemed to want this when we were married either. And now I'm alone and I can't finish my book and no one wants anything I have to offer, because I have nothing."

I'm standing in front of my ex-husband in my bra and underwear, and they don't even match.

Before I can look up at him, Dawson was inches from my face, his right hand went on my waist and the other on my cheek and his lips found mine as though he was a bee and I was the pollen. He kissed me like when we first started dating. My heart raced, and I wanted to push him away, but I couldn't because I missed this. He was always a great kisser. Finally, he did it for me and pulled his lips from mine. I stumbled. I caught my breath and pressed my lips together, still tasting him on them.

"No, Analena, you're mistaken. I never stopped wanting this." He stepped back and his hands fell from my body. "Just because things ended in divorce doesn't mean I stopped wanting you. Remember, you asked for the divorce. But damn, you have to love yourself for once in your life, because you never did when we were together. And that's what is preventing others from loving you now."

Dawson swiped his keys off the coffee table. "And stop hiding away inside this condo. I know how you get. You form habits, and you don't allow yourself to live." He kissed my forehead as I pulled up my pants, and by the time my shirt was on, the front door closed with him on the other side of it.

Gosh, I hated when he was right, which wasn't often, and usually at the most inconvenient of times.

Chapter 18

Now fully clothed again, I flopped onto the couch and grabbed my wineglass. My mind fumbled like a VHS tape that had been recorded over too many times as I grappled with what had occurred minutes ago. How could Dawson love me at my worst when I didn't love him like he loved me? And that kiss. I swigged a gulp of wine. I missed the romance. I missed the closeness and having someone desire to be with me. And while Dawson wanted to be that someone, I didn't want him. I also missed loving myself yet had no way of figuring out how to do that again.

Tears filled my eyelids. I just wanted to feel better about myself. Maybe it was time to learn to accept who I was and not try to change. Love through acceptance. I'd not been happy in some time, when I should be, especially now that I was following my dream. It should have flipped the switch.

I glanced around the room. I needed to make a change, embrace my flaws and focus on what I had. Learn to love who I was and where I was.

After all, it was Christmas Eve, and I had no problem with Dawson being right about my holiday traditions. In some regards, traditions were the true meaning of Christmas.

"It's time to make my cheese pizza." I pulled up the internet on my cell phone and searched for homemade pizza recipes. I should have most of what I needed. The grocery store would be closed, so I would make do either way. Then, I searched for where I could stream *Home Alone*.

The joy of Christmas spread through me instantly, and I was overtaken with nostalgia as though I were younger. I smiled and rushed to the kitchen, pulling out the flour. "Crap, no yeast." I searched for pizza recipes without yeast. "Yes!"

Then I froze. The pit of my stomach hurt thinking about whatever Dawson would be doing now. Waiting at the airport, back at his hotel, if he had even booked one. Then I thought about it more, on a deeper pinot-gris-fueled level. "What was wrong with wanting to be alone? What was wrong with not figuring it all out? What was wrong with failure? This was *my* year of new things, not anyone else's."

Thankfully, I located baking soda in the cupboard, far past the best-by date, but those were just suggestions. I had spaghetti sauce and cheddar cheese. I scooped out the flour and then added the water. The recipe was not typical, but I didn't have the ingredients I needed, and I wanted pizza. I needed pizza. "What could go wrong?"

I crossed my arms and tilted my head at the pizza I'd just pulled out of the oven. It was more of a heart shape with a burned left side, and it turns out that expired baking soda does matter. The crust was as flat as a stop sign.

"Darn you, Pinterest!" I held both fists up in the air.

My phone rang, and I was sure to check this time to see whose name appeared.

"Merry Christmas, Amy!" I cheered in the direction of the phone that I placed on speaker.

"I'm so sorry, Rob spilled the beans. Are you okay? What happened." Amy's voice was an octave higher than normal.

"Yes." I glanced at the pizza. "I already sent him on his way, after I bared my soul while stripping down in front of him."

"You did what?"

"You know me and my struggles with feeling needed and attractive. So, I bared most of my body."

"Oh no, Analena."

"I was nice enough to leave on my mismatched granny panties and three-year-old bra."

"Yikes. So, you're not okay. Give me Tape Measure Man's number. I'll make sure he turns your frown right-side up."

I looked at the pizza and then at the tiny tree. "You know I'm actually okay. I have some really friendly neighbors, and Tape Measure Man and I have a date—plan, I meant *plan* for tomorrow morning. Stupid pinot."

"I knew it." Amy laughed, and then I heard a commotion in the background, the girls and her husband making noise. "Thanks for calling. I know you're busy with the family traditions."

"Never too busy to wish you a Merry Christmas. And best of luck with Tape Measure Man and whatever non-date-date you have planned."

I grinned like the Grinch. "Merry Christmas."

"Merry Christmas."

The line went dead, and I was once again alone. "Pizza time."

I took a knife because I couldn't find a pizza slicer and cut triangles into the crunchy bread. Pizza should never be cut into squares. Then I slid it onto the plate, topped off my wineglass, and carried them to the couch. I wished I had some small lights. The tree is nice, but there was something about the warm glow of light that really made it feel like Christmas.

I rested the plate on my lap and wiggled back into the couch cushions. I hit a few buttons on the remote and brought up *Home Alone*. The start of the movie always gave me warm fuzzies and I think about the first time I saw it. The theater had been packed, the air held the smell of buttered popcorn and sweets, and my sneakers stuck to the soda-covered floors. Everyone was eager to see the movie. Gosh, I missed those years; life was so different and wonderful. Now there was little excitement in our current world of want it, get it, no wait time needed. The only thing people really waited for was a book release, and even that could be arranged to get it sooner with so many advanced reader copies that go out to try to get early reviews. In the end, how many are still waiting?

I chomped on the pizza and paused, expecting it to be horrible. It was not great. It was doable for my tradition. And right now, it's what I needed because I missed so many things. I missed my best friend, being in my actual home, being around others and part of a community, and I missed being in a relationship. Todd was right, and Dawson knew it. Without having seen me in months, I'd really isolated myself. But at this point, time was running away from me as I chased after my dream.

I mouthed every line from *Home Alone* aloud and still laughed at the same old silliness. Then something outside caught my eye. Christmas lights in the distance.

I set the plate down and eased toward the slider as though it were a hovering UFO. I pulled open the door and stepped out onto the patio. The chill cooled my wine-flushed face instantly. "It's a sailboat, with lights."

The saltiness and dampness of the weather wrapped around me. I took a few more steps and shouted, "Merry Christmas!"

I felt funny and shook my head.

"Merry Christmas, Nevada," a male voice came from my left, a few patios down.

"Mason, I'm sorry I didn't see you there."

"No worries. I just stepped outside. Hank comes by every year, as long as the weather is right, and sails his boat along the shore for everyone who's looking."

"That's really nice of him." I wrapped my arms around myself, as my teeth chattered.

"Are you having a nice Christmas Eve?"

I glanced back inside. "I am. Different, but somewhat traditional."

"Good, very good. Look, I wanted to say I'm sorry about the way I've been acting standoffish around you. I misjudged you."

"Thank you, I appreciate it. But I saw where you were coming from. There are a lot of people out there who have a very easy life. Those who get everything handed to them. While others have to take the hard road, sometimes with never-ending switchbacks. It's hard not to envy what others have, especially if it's something you want."

"Well, even though I'm an old fart, I should behave better. Have a nice rest of your Christmas Eve, Nevada."

"Merry Christmas, Mason."

I turned back and headed inside but stayed at the slider and watched Hank's boat until I couldn't see it anymore. I guess in a new and unexpected way, I did get my glowing Christmas lights after all.

Chapter 19

Even though it was thirty-five degrees outside, the palms of my hands were sweating, and my heart raced. In my hands was my traditional, but odd, Christmas morning snack, along with a bottle of chardonnay.

Todd's door flung open, and he stood there, wearing blue pajama bottoms with outlines of dog faces on them. Todd looked so cozy that I wanted to snuggle up against him like he was a blanket.

I peered over him.

"What are you looking for up there?" Todd gazed up at the ceiling.

"I don't know where tall people hide things, like extra pets."

"Last time I checked not above us."

"You promise Whidbey is—"

"A good dog? Yes, I promise."

I huffed. "Whidbey is *locked up.*"

"Merry Christmas, Analena. And no, he's not locked up. He's not a prisoner. But he's in his crate for now. Oh, what do you have in there?" He pointed at my container.

"Are you sure we don't want to do this at my place?"

"No, my TV's bigger." Todd took my arm and pulled me inside, shutting the door behind me.

I'd not been in his condo before. It had dark bluish-gray walls covered in framed black-and-white historic home photographs. The fireplace crackled, and Whidbey sat upright in his crate at the side of the kitchen. His tail thumped against it, making a racket. Even though the dog was secure, I held back, as though he could open the crate door and leap out. He quickly returned to lying down, biting into a Santa stuffed toy.

There was a worn brown leather couch, and the massive TV mounted on the wall played a Christmas movie that within a few seconds I could determine was clearly a romantic comedy.

"That TV is huge!" I handed Todd the bottle of wine.

"Morning drinker?"

"No, I guess I felt odd coming over without something festively adult-like." I checked my watch. "It's almost ten thirty, some may consider it close enough to noon."

"Are you that someone?"

"Depends on the day."

Todd laughed. "I'm glad you wore your pajamas. Or I'd feel ridiculous." He carried the chardonnay to the kitchen island. "So, tell me, what's in the bowl?"

"Puppy chow."

Todd froze; his eyes questioned me. "The woman who is afraid of anything with fur made a snack called puppy chow?"

"I didn't name it. It's been a tradition since I was a kid."

"Hopefully, your mix goes well with assorted cheeses, crackers, and meats. Because"—he points to the platter on the countertop—"this is my go-to for Christmas."

"I love nothing more than assorted meats and cheeses. Looks great." I set the bowl of sugary goodness on the kitchen counter and stood across from Todd. I couldn't help staring at him, thinking about how attractive I found him, taking in all his qualities. I was surprised I wasn't dizzy from all my racing thoughts.

"Did you have a nice Christmas Eve?" Todd popped the cork on the wine.

"It was . . . unexpected." I tried not to wince. I wasn't sure I wanted to mention the ex-husband's surprise visit. I was still trying to figure out how I felt about the entire thing.

"Did you see Hank's sailboat?"

"Oh, yes. What about you?"

"I got wrapped up in a holiday rom-com movie marathon last night and completely missed it."

"Why are you being wrapped up in romantic comedies?" I felt butterflies develop in my stomach, something I hadn't felt in years.

"Why are you not? I prefer lighter, uplifting movies. The ones that don't remind me about the world outside my front door. Don't get me wrong, I love old classics, westerns and action, of course, mysteries. I'm not really into the horror, sci-fi scene. What about you?"

"I love scary movies. Actually, horror is probably my favorite." I smirked. "But of course at Christmastime I enjoy pretty much anything holiday themed." The smells of the meat and cheese assortment in front of me caused my mouth to water. "So how do you handle Christmas when you don't have Dylan on the actual day? Do you celebrate before or after?" I noticed the tree all lit up in the corner by the slider and the string of lights over the fireplace mantel with what appeared to be an empty stocking with Dylan's name sewn into it, next to one with Whidbey stitched in it.

Todd removed two wineglasses from the cupboard and motioned with them to the couch. I skirted the wall as I made my way by the dog crate, giving it a wide berth. Whidbey's eyes followed me, and then his stately body spun around, bumping the crate, causing it to shake. I landed on the couch and grabbed a throw pillow as though it were a knight's shield.

"Dylan doesn't grasp the concept of Christmas or any of the associated activities such as opening presents. He's usually glued to his tablet, so I just keep his subscriptions current on his favorite shows and channels. I attempted the whole stocking thing, but trying to get his attention to explain what the stocking was about didn't work. It broke my heart that it never clicked for him."

"I'm sorry. I shouldn't have asked. It's really none of my business."

"Nonsense, it's just part of being a parent. Autistic or not, nothing really ever goes as planned." He set the platter on the coffee table, along with my puppy chow, and then returned with the wineglasses, bottle, and salad plates. "How's the book going?"

"I'm less than a quarter of the way done with the first draft."

"So, is that three-sixteenths, one-eighth, or one-sixteenth?"

I gaped at him. "What?"

"You said less than a quarter."

"Don't math me on Christmas."

Todd's eyes squinched. "Math you?"

"Yes, you're doing your tape measure thing. It involves math, and I don't do math."

"Math is not something you do. It's part of life. It's usable."

"Yes, for baking and cooking."

"There you go." He leaned forward and loaded his plate with cheese.

"No, I don't do math outside of the kitchen."

He tossed a cube of cheese into his mouth. "You're probably one-sixteenth. You're pushing it close for your goal of finishing the first draft by New Year's Eve."

"I'm shockingly aware. I'm stuck. Frustratingly stuck and the T key still won't put any ink on the page. Every paragraph I write seems horrible, the storyline feels weak, and the characters come off as flat. I'm wasting my time. I want to give up because I can't figure out what's making me feel that way about the story. It sucks to feel you're failing at your dream."

"I know, but you're not."

Whidbey laid down in the crate, taking the Santa back into his mouth, and let out a long sigh. We turned our attention to the Christmas movie as we munched away on our snacks and sipped wine, but I couldn't focus, and I stared off into space.

"Get up," Todd said.

I turned to him. "What?" I assumed I'd spilled something, so I inspected around me. "Sorry, I'm going to focus on the movie. I didn't mean to ruin this."

"We're getting you out of here."

I set my empty plate on the coffee table. "I didn't mean to zone out."

Todd took my hand and pulled me to a standing position. "That's why we need to go. What was I thinking? Having you come over, you're just moving from one inside to another inside. You need to get some fresh air."

"Open a window." I motioned toward the living room one.

"You need to stretch your legs."

"But it's cold outside. I'm from Nevada, remember, and the section that stays mostly warm, the one closest to Arizona. *The desert.*"

"Nice try, you loved the snow. Which happens when it's cold. You need to get out of your head."

"No, I'm okay."

"No, you're not."

"I'm in my pajamas."

"No one is out today. It'll just be us and Whidbey."

I shook my head as my eyes widened. "I can't go with Whidbey."

Todd glanced at the dog and then back at me. "It'll break his heart not to go."

I eyed Whidbey and then Todd, who wore the best puppy-dog sad face ever. "Nope, sorry, I just can't. He could eat me."

Todd laughed. "He can't eat you. He's not a bear. He's a German shepherd."

"He looks as big as a bear. He's like a mixed brown-and-black bear with his color."

Todd glanced at Whidbey. "Maybe a cub, and just as cute."

I crossed my arms and huffed.

"Okay, fine, I can take him out later."

"Thank you."

"You need a jacket. Meet me outside in two minutes."

A few minutes later, I'm wearing a jacket, gloves, and sneakers.

"Is that all you have for footwear?" Todd pointed as soon as he spotted me.

"I wasn't really planning for any wet excursions." I smirked.

"Good point. We can warm up your feet by the fire when we get back." Todd's face still had a sad puppy-dog look about him.

My heart twitched thinking about poor lonely Whidbey locked in his crate on Christmas Day. "Go get him." I motioned my hand up the flight of stairs.

Todd turned around and looked back up at his condo. "Whidbey?"

"Yes, but you better keep him far far away from me. I mean, on the other side of your body but even further."

"I'll be right back." Todd took the steps in twos.

I waited, and when he returned with the bear-cop dog, I kept my distance. "Why does he look bigger out here?"

"He should look smaller." Todd paused. "I guess, to be fair, you're both the same height, so I can understand where you're coming from."

"Does that mean you're besties with Bigfoot? Because you're both shockingly tall."

"He prefers to be called Biggie. That's his nickname when we go camping."

"Hilarious," I deadpanned, and I followed behind him at a bus length's distance. "Where are we going?"

"We're exploring, which means walking."

"When you said explore, I thought you meant a nice warm drive."

"So, you can go from inside the condo to inside the truck? No."

We walked along a path that led to an area of water where a bunch of wooden poles poked out of the water. I'm instantly ashamed that while I came here to write, I've not done anything but go to and from the library, grocery store, and an occasional stroll half a mile down the beach.

Even on a rare sunny day, I hide out. My skin looks like I've been living in Ireland this entire time.

Todd slowed his pace so my short legs could keep up with his longer legs. I desperately want our jackets to rub up against each other because I wanted to be close to him. But the dog, although busy sniffing and ignoring me completely, is still too close. I continued to follow behind like a straggling kid kicking rocks. But craving conversation, I scurried forward yet remained at a horizontal distance because of Whidbey.

"How's it going being here alone, I mean without a spouse?" Todd finally said, breaking the silence between us and the noisy shore.

"It's not hard, but different, sort of an out-of-body feeling at times. I think the marriage was hard enough that when it ended, it was more a weight lifted off my shoulders. As though I had freedom to really live life to the fullest. Not that I have yet to do that, even so, I had the option. I think that's why it feels awkward when someone asks me if I want to get married again. Maybe it's not meant for me. Like maybe I'm not good enough to marry, to be a wife again."

"Doesn't sound like it, just sounds like he wasn't the right match for you. Divorce, even if agreed upon, is never easy."

"It was as though I'd just cleaned my closet and got rid of all the things that no longer suited me."

"Ouch," Todd mouthed. "So, is that why you took a sabbatical to write your novel? Because you discovered your dreams in the back of the closet?"

"Writing a novel had been a goal of mine since I was in my twenties. I never planned on being a grocery store cashier, let alone getting divorced. But he's just been hanging on."

"Not a good thing for him, but I'm sure it's nice knowing he's not over you. That you're special enough for him to still want it to work with you."

"I would prefer that he completely moves on."

"Do you think people who divorce completely move on?"

I followed Todd to the shore, and in front of us was a series of rocks, covered in algae and crusty scales. We were the only ones on the shore.

"For the most part, I would think so, hope so. Life is about moving forward, and that involves moving on." I'd stepped closer to Todd and thus to Whidbey and had to catch myself.

His eyes gazed out into the distance, his hand on the leash. "I think there is always a part of you that is left behind, even if you move on. You always leave a mark wherever you've been. And in a way, it helps form your future. You just said so yourself."

I tripped over a piece of seaweed but caught myself. "I did."

"Come with me." Todd waved me toward the edge that led to a strip of wet sand and then another, large rock formation.

"I can't get any closer. My feet are already frozen." I checked my zipper to make sure it was up to my chin. "And you have Whidbey."

"But you need to."

"Whatever you need to show me, I can see it from here." I clenched my teeth. The breeze off the ocean was chilly.

"Nope." Todd circled Whidbey's leash around an enormous chunk of driftwood and tugged it tight to check it was secure.

He held out his gloved hand. "Let's go."

"It's a slippery rock."

He raised his eyebrow and kept his hand stretched outwards.

I huffed. "Fine!" I moved forward, my sneakers sinking into the wet sand. My hand found his, and he held up some of my weight as I climbed the few steps to the top.

Standing at the top of the boulder, I looked around. To my left and right, massive waves crashed into the land and the other rocks.

"Close your eyes," Todd said and kept hold of my hand. His other hand touched my waist as he moved next to me.

"You're not going to push me off, are you?"

"No, I don't want to mess up the ocean with blood."

I eyed him. "Okay, but all it will do is make me dizzy."

"I've got you. Now. What do you hear? What do you smell? What do you feel?"

I took another deep breath that caused me to feel off balance, and I leaned into Todd's hands. "Seagulls. Salty air. Moisture on my skin."

"And do you know why you feel those?"

"Because you made me come out here?"

Todd laughed, and when I opened my eyes, I saw him smirking.

"What?" I grabbed his arm as I began sliding.

He held me tight, and I rebalanced myself. "No, you're experiencing those things because you're present in the moment. You're focused on now. You're not trying to create that image later in a story."

"But I know what the ocean is. I know what it looks like and feels like."

"Of course you do, from memory, but what about from the here and now? The current current." Todd chuckled. "With each day that passes, we see things differently. Our perspective changes or at least can shift. I always used to think my childhood home was massive. Every room was huge. A few years ago, it was listed for sale, and I went and did a tour. It was nothing like I remembered. My bedroom, small; the tree out back with the tire, it was older and taller, but in my memory, it was twice as tall and wide."

"Because you were once smaller."

"True, but also everything looked different. Some things had changed but the entire experience in driving down the street, into the neighborhood, and then the house, helped me notice that our views, our beliefs, our vision, our understanding, our likes, dislikes are always up for re-discovery. Just like divorce, as you mentioned, things move forward, change, reshape who we are."

I continued looking into the ocean's waves, the foam at the edges of the water, and the cloudy sky turning a light shade of blue between the layers. He was right. My writing was stagnant because I'd become stagnant. I was sadder, not happier.

"Do you want to head back? I don't want your toes to freeze and fall off." Todd looked at my soaking wet sneakers.

"I'm sure a few more minutes wouldn't matter."

Chapter 20

Winter

That day with Todd turned into the most important day of my novel year so far. I didn't know if it had been spending time with him, or if something in the holiday air had caused the shift. Maybe even having things pointed out to me by two men, one who knew me well and one who was getting to know me, was enough of a wake-up call since they were unknowingly on the same page.

The rain drizzled down the window at the library, creating the most perfect scene for working on my mystery story. I'd been there for several hours chipping away at edits for some of the chapters I'd typed up, marking up the pages with purple arrows and notes in the margins like I used to do in high school. I'd already filled up the page, so I was stuck with shoving the edits in random places. Of course, this wayward approach to editing ended up costing me more time. It was a bad plan from the beginning, causing me to do extra work. What was I thinking? Typing it up old-school, plus a fresh copy for edits just meant double the work when I could have added it directly into the computer.

Today, the library was not busy, but the atmosphere was lively between the staff and patrons that lingered around the shelves. The few children who came in with their parents to read were in the children's corner.

I drew from the energy, especially when I didn't have much left in my fingers as they cramped. I took in random strangers' body language, outfits, and the way they communicated, infusing it into my manuscript notes. Right now, I was down to what I hoped were the final two chapters of the first draft, and New Year's Eve was tomorrow. If all the stars aligned, I would hit my personal deadline, and finally be able to type THE END. Although it would come out as HE END thanks to my broken T key. I couldn't wait! That would give me two months to work on revisions and rewrites, with a completed second draft by February.

Christmas decorations still hung from the library's windows, and even though it was only three thirty in the afternoon, darkness filled the sky by the second. I'd need to do better with my time management for the edits.

Focus. I returned to my manuscript and read the next paragraph, checking for anything that needed fixing.

```
It was not that I didn't hear the
scream, more that I couldn't make out
         who it belonged to.
```

The lights went off and on overhead, and Wendy, the librarian, walked over.

"Analena, so sorry, but we're closing early. With all the rain on the road and the freezing temperatures setting in, black ice is going to be bad." Wendy wrapped her heather gray cardigan tighter. "Are you at a good stopping point?"

"I can be." I began loading up my supplies and manuscript into my shoulder bag.

"Be sure to pick up some of Nancy's homemade toffee on your way out. She left some little bags by the checkout." Wendy smiled.

"Thank you." I dropped my purple pen into the bag. "Have a great New Year's."

"You as well, Analena."

As I passed by the circulation desk, I tossed a bag of toffee into my purse and made my way to the car. After climbing inside, I pulled out a piece of toffee and slid it into my mouth. Its caramel goodness warmed me from the inside out, and then I crunched.

"Oh, no," I mumbled. "My tooth!"

This was not part of my plan. I chipped something. The pain shot down into my jaw. After locating the only dental office nearby on my cell phone, I started the car.

The darkness of the evening made it hard for me to find the small dental office, Ocean Cove Dental, at the edge of town. So, after nearly sliding into a stop sign, I made a U-turn and spotted the jumbo toothbrush holding up the weathered white sign.

With my hand pressed to the right side of my chin, I reached for the front door as it flung open. A man in his late thirties wearing a heavy jacket and beanie appeared. What was with all the men my age in this town being so darn attractive?

"Sorry, we called all remaining patients to let them know we're closing because of the threat of ice." He looked at me, my hand on my chin. "I don't recognize you."

"I'm not an atient," I enunciated poorly. "Atient."

He squinted his eyes. "Oh, you're not a patient of Doctor Taylor."

I shook my head. The pain was much worse standing in the cold air. "Emergency. Had offee."

"Toffee, oh no, well, come in. The doctor just left, but I'm his hygienist, Chad Billingsly." He held open the door, and I followed him inside, along with a gust of wind.

"Ou of ate insurance." I remain standing, now in the small living room, because the dental office was clearly once a house.

"We don't accept out-of-state insurance. We accept cash."

I frowned.

"Credit cards too." Chad tilted his head. "Post-dated checks."

I nodded and tried to smile but gave him a thumbs-up instead. He showed me to a plastic-covered chair and hit the lights. The room came to life. The chair faced a window, and the walls were covered in photos of tropical ocean waves.

"Now, let's have a look." Chad motioned to the seat as he washed his hands in the small sink behind the chair.

I eased onto the pale-tan lounge chair, still holding my mouth. He pulled on some blue gloves with a snap at his wrist and then added some goofy-looking spectacles. He grabbed the overhead light and shone it into my mouth.

After what felt like an hour of my mouth being ajar, when it was probably less than a minute, Chad said, "Well, we're going to need the doctor for this one. You chipped a crown."

I closed my eyes and let out a whine.

"It's a whole process to remove the broken crown, put a temporary one on while the new one gets made and then set it." Chad rolled himself back onto the circle padded chair and pushed the glasses off his nose.

"I fon't nee his righ now." I pushed my head into the chair's headrest and brought both hands to my eyes.

"Don't worry about that, Doctor Taylor is the best."

"How much ill his coss?"

Chad removed the gloves and motioned for me to follow him back to the waiting area where he slid behind the desk and punched keys on the laptop. He glanced up over the laptop and clenched his teeth, showing their whiteness. "A thousand twenty-three."

"Oh, whoa." I slumped over.

Of course, just when everything was moving in the right direction, life had dropped a big roadblock right in front of me in the shape of toffee.

Chapter 21

My dental care ended up costing more than money out of my limited saving, it cost me time, too. Time I didn't have to waste. I even missed out on the New Year's Eve celebration because of the pain. Plus, there was an appointment to prepare the tooth, and then I had to come back in for the crown, and the pain halted my writing. If I were in pain, I couldn't write, and if I took the pain medication, my thoughts were hazy. The month of January was all but done with, and I had barely made a dent in my first round of edits to the manuscript.

The rain pelted the side of the slider as though it was planning an attack. I wrapped my hands around a coffee mug; the steam from the black liquid rose. Having had the crown put on only a week ago, my mouth was still a little sore, but I was getting back into the habit of chewing on both sides of my mouth again.

I stared at the stack of written pages on the desk and thought about how I'd promised myself that I'd get out at least for daily morning walks, but that usually ended up being only once a week. I'd also promised Todd I'd go out on some form of adventure twice a month. It didn't have to cost much other than gas. Pack a lunch, hop in the car, and drive to some place nearby that sounded or looked interesting. But my broken tooth got me out of that for the last few weeks. Plus, it helped that Todd had been gone pretty much nonstop for the month on a special work project. Hopefully, he'd forgotten about this two-pronged pet plan.

I looked around the dreary condo. There was nothing worth watching on TV, as I'd burned through all my shows as soon as they were released. I'd even grabbed two books from the community library and already finished them.

I sipped coffee, wondering about the shelves at the community building. Maybe I could find a few more gems. Glancing down at my body, I was guilt riddled. I should go work out, not find more ways to sit around. My weight was so frustrating. How was a writer expected to write a book if they had to get ten thousand steps a day? *Treadmill desk.*

I briefly debated putting on workout clothes but ended up reasoning that tomorrow was Monday, so I could dive back into a routine then. I huffed and bundled myself up as though I were going to step outside into the Alaskan wilderness. Once the dampness got into my bones, it took a hot shower to get it out.

Once outside, I rationalized that even the trip across the parking lot would be enough for today's workout. The wind made every step a challenge, and the rain felt like ice shards cutting my face. I shivered as I slid the key into the lock of the community building and welcomed the warmth inside.

The gym lights were off, but the main lights were on. It must have been the sudden shift in temperatures playing tricks on me because something blurry, blackish, and fuzzy was moving towards the bookcase.

"Hello?" I asked, taking a few steps towards the back of the couch that sat in front of the bookcases.

The blinds were open, filtering only a little light with the heavy rain outside. I heard something move from behind me, and when I glanced back toward the bookcase, a book slid forward on the shelf. I gripped the couch as the book fell to the floor.

I screamed and wrapped my arms around myself. "Maybe I do need to get out more."

I turned on a light that shone directly onto the shelf, but it revealed nothing unusual. Making my way to the fallen book, I slowly picked it up and glanced around the room. I went to put the book back on the shelf but when I flipped it over, the title caught my eye. *Your Survival Instinct Is Killing You: Retrain Your Brain to Conquer Fear and Build Resilience.* I almost dropped the book.

I spun around. "Very funny."

But the building was silent.

I slid the book back into the spot it had fallen from and continued to scan the shelves. The selection of books leaned heavily into the Fabio era of romance and Tom Clancy thrillers. I avoided anything with a pink spine or the word *lust* in the title. I grabbed a black-spined book with bold white print, flipping it over to find a photo of the author covering the entire back cover. Wondering what my author photo would look like, I pulled another book forward as though it unlocked a hidden passageway. This too had an author photo, but it was a newer book since it didn't take up the entire back. Jealously twinkled in my eyes. When would I get my author photos? I shoved the books into the crook of my arm. I reached for one more as a chill encapsulated my arm, and I paused. A white spine book has slid out about half an inch from the rest. It was the fallen book I'd put back. I swear I pushed it all the way in, making it flush with the rest.

"Alright, I guess I'll get this book too." I removed it from the shelf.

I admired the three books, fanning the pages, the scent of aged, yellowing paper flitting into my nostrils. Running my hands over the cover, the debossed letters were like brail under my fingertips. Tears welled in my eyes, and I knew it was stupid. It was childish. It was almost certainly perimenopause mixed with the failure I felt so far. I wanted to hold a book of my own, to see my name, my words, to see the world I created on the pages. To see my name on the cover of a novel that was worn from being shoved into a purse, or that sat dog-eared on a nightstand, or that hid a face on the subway. I envisioned myself at a book signing, lines of readers giddy to meet me. The thing about my dream was that it felt possible when I was dreaming it, but now that I was living it, the outcome felt as though it was drifting further away.

As I headed for the door, I remembered Todd's story about ghosts. But I didn't believe in ghosts. As a child, I never feared the monsters under my bed. I never really believed in anything—Santa, the Easter Bunny, finding Prince Charming—and right now I didn't believe I could make it through the first round of revisions.

I covered the books as I made my way back to the condo. Somehow the rain seemed sharper now, as though there was anger in the drops. I made it to the first-floor landing when I heard, "Hey."

I looked up to find Todd and Whidbey standing in front of me, the rain slanted against the wind.

"Todd." I huddled the books closer to my chest to protect them from the rain.

But before I could say anything, Piepie clomped down the stairs in sunflower-yellow galoshes and a matching raincoat, holding one of her dogs, not the black bear one, who was also in a matching yellow outfit.

"This weather is giving me depression," Piepie said, reaching the end of the steps. "I'm super late for Marshall's spa day, but Analena, we must get together again. It's been too long. The chocolate martinis are calling our names."

I nodded. "Yes, that would be fun."

"Hi, Whidbey, how are you?" Piepie paused, Marshall resting comfortably in her arms. "Todd, don't let me forget to get you those homemade dog T-R-E-A-T-S."

"Will do." He nodded, switching the leash to his other hand.

Piepie scurried to her SUV and disappeared inside.

"Why did she spell treat?" I asked, turning around to Todd.

That's when everything went haywire. Whidbey lunged; his leash taut at the end of Todd's hand whipped forward. I clutched the books even tighter and squeezed my eyes as Whidbey leaped. His paws bounced off my stomach, his tongue on my chin. I screamed as though a python had been thrown at me.

"Whidbey, down," Todd's voice came through the panic. "Are you okay, Analena?"

My heart was racing so fast, I could feel the blood pumping rapidly up and down my body. I was no longer cold. I was breathing heavily, or maybe I was trying to catch my breath, I wasn't sure.

"Analena? Are you okay?" Todd's hand found my shoulder.

I swallowed. "He tried to kill me!"

"No, he jumped on you. He wasn't holding a knife. I think you're overreacting a bit."

I looked down. I seemed alright, nothing hurt, but my heartbeat was still thumping loudly in my ears. Whidbey let out a whine from where he was sitting.

"See, he's sorry. He didn't mean to scare you." Todd motioned with his head toward Whidbey. "You can't say the T-word. He sort of freaks out. To be fair, most dogs do. Sorry he jumped on you, though. He should know better." Todd shook my shoulder. "Analena, you're okay."

I pushed the emotions forming into the back of my throat. "No, I'm not. I told you dogs are dangerous. And for the record, I was not overreacting."

"He's not part of the mob. He was just excited. I'm sorry, honestly. He wasn't going to eat you or bite you. Whidbey does it to me all the time when he's excited. I should be better at teaching him, but he likes to dance with me, so he's used to putting his paws on me."

I backed away, heading toward my condo's door. "Whatever pronged plan you thought you had with getting me to be okay with dogs will never happen now." I shoved the key into the lock and didn't even turn around when I slammed the door.

Chapter 22

I couldn't help but feel sadness when I stared at the date on my cell phone's lock screen. Today I turned forty. But there wouldn't be cake in the break room or sparkling apple cider and a group-signed birthday card. Today, I'd be alone.

Amy had called and sung deafeningly into the video chat. But something still felt amiss. Not that getting older was something to be eager about. I mean, things just start breaking down and hurting for no reason. While each year is an accomplishment, it differed greatly from turning sixteen, eighteen, or twenty-one. Maybe if they made cards that didn't make old people jokes once you reached a certain age, then you'd want to blow out your candles with a smile.

Even though I was trying my best not to focus on my weight loss, I stepped on the scale to torture myself this morning. My weight was the same as it was two weeks ago, when I should have been down at least a pound with my calorie restriction and gym workouts. "Well now. I guess eating cake won't matter. So, that's a plus."

Although Dawson and I were never big on birthdays, he always made an effort to take me out to dinner at my favorite restaurant and splurge on wine and dessert. A simple chocolate fudge cake with a topping of fresh raspberries was just the ticket. "With a traditional buttercream frosting," I said aloud in a British accent that would cause Paul Hollywood to give that trademark smirk.

I shook my head. No, I was supposed to be writing, as I was still muddling through round one of revisions. I'd have to buy a cake. Otherwise, this would end up like the last three attempts to write today. It was only eleven in the morning, and I'd cleaned the bathroom, painted my fingernails and toenails in a moody blue to match the never-ending gloomy weather, and fallen down the rabbit hole of '90s where-are-they-now celebrities. I had to edit at least one chapter, and then I would allow myself to run to the grocery store and pick up a slice or, let's face it, maybe a whole chocolate cake.

I took my coffee cup to the desk and prepared the stack of papers for the next chapter, to type into the Word document. Sadly, my typing skills had not gotten better since computer class in middle school.

Outside, the morning sun was behind the condo, and the sky was a mix of gray clouds. The waves crashed along the shore as the seagulls squawked, their feathers reflecting the sunlight with each flyby. I often found myself staring at them as I zoned out, seconds giving way to minutes.

"Focus. It's only a chapter." I wiggled in the patio chair to sit up straight and prepared my fingers over the mini keyboard attached to my tablet.

```
No matter how much I would love to
  tell you that August had two evil
stepsisters, she lost her glass shoe,
and Prince Charming found her in the
end, that is not this story. While it
 is a story about a stepmother-step-
daughter relationship, I think that
```

```
August would have preferred to have
been Cinderella. I would also love to
tell you that she lived in the castle,
whether it be in the basement or up in
the tower, but she lived in a trailer.
I will say, however, it was one of
those nice trailers; you know, the
double-wide kind with a small flower
              garden outside.
```

I leaned back in the chair. "Not bad."

Returning to the story, I focused and finished typing the chapter within a half hour.

"Cake time!" I cheered.

I changed out of my pajamas, grabbed my coat, and headed for the front door. When I swung open the door, Piepie's fist was coming at my face.

"Analena!" She cheered and put her hand down.

My eyes scanned her for pets. "Hey, Piepie. I was just heading out. Did you need something?"

"I was coming to see if you wanted to join me for lunch, remember we mentioned doing it again. There is a new bistro restaurant that opened up one town over." Piepie smiled. "To be honest, I could really use a break from pet-mom duty and some woman-to-woman conversation. Frank is getting tired of listening to me when he's trying to relax and talk to those people on his ham radio."

I noticed a piece of straw in her curls and fished it out, holding it up for her to see.

"It's everywhere. You'd think I roll around with them in their cages."

I laughed. "Actually, it's my birthday, so that sounds great. But if you don't mind, I'd like to take separate cars. I need to run to the grocery store afterwards."

"Your birthday? Then we must!" She wrapped me in a hug. "Happy birthday, girl! And no worries, I need to go get more feed from the pet supply store out in Crooked River." Piepie pulled out her cell from her purse. "The place is called Cove Bistro, off 58th and Main."

"Great, I'll see you there," I said as I locked my front door.

The Cove Bistro was crowded, but the layout made for easy navigation to a booth along the far wall. Modern beach décor of pale blues and worn golds allowed for a relaxed vibe. The server handed us a crisp menu, without the grease stains that would undoubtedly appear in a few months.

"Everything sounds yummy." Piepie's face was completely hidden behind the menu, her voice coming over the top. "Let's get something fun to drink, birthday girl."

"Fun?"

"Lavender lemonade."

"That sounds good."

We put in our orders, and Piepie pulled out a twenty-dollar bill. She smoothed it out on the table between us. I looked at it and then back at her.

"I must tell you this incredible story." Piepie pressed her hand against the twenty. "I can't tell Frank, or my sister or parents. They'd never believe me. But I feel as though you're open-minded and . . . well, do you believe in God or a higher power?

I shrugged my shoulders. "I pray, sometimes."

"Okay, I can work with that. So, I was out walking in front of these houses in the neighborhood across from the condos the other night. It was getting darker every minute, and the visibility was almost gone. I came upon a wadded-up twenty-dollar bill on the sidewalk. It was between a parked car and the path to a home's front door. I assumed it belonged to someone who just ran inside the house and it had fallen from their pocket. I didn't want to take someone's money. I prayed to God that the person missing this would find it. I wasn't bold enough to assume that it belonged to someone who lived there. Maybe it was a fellow walker, and they would come back and check. I told God that I'm so grateful to be rich that I can pass by a twenty and leave it. Which is not the case, but you know, positivity." Piepie wiggled her fingers in a half jazz-hands way. "So, the next day I'm out walking in the same neighborhood, but now I'm about five houses down from where that twenty was. Then I looked down, and something was blowing my way. And wouldn't you know, I take a few steps and spot a wadded-up twenty. No one is around, and I'm not in front of anyone's home."

"You think it was the same twenty?"

"It was wadded up exactly the same way. But I mean a whole day went by, and I've seen people walking up and down that sidewalk, and no one picked it up."

"But you did, right? That's the twenty?"

"Darn straight. I took it as God telling me since I didn't take it originally that he gave it to me. Now I suppose it could fall under positive manifestation. But any way you slice that cake, I still got a piece. It was literally handed to me."

I pondered her story. "Do you think that positivity will help me get through my edits?"

Piepie smiled. "It's a start at least."

I hinted at a smile. "Well then, no harm in trying."

Chapter 23

I'd given a lot of thought to Piepie's amazing bout of luck. And throughout the entire drive from the bistro to the grocery store and then home, I asked whoever was listening—God, or maybe his assistant—to provide me with some type of guidance for the rest of my novel year. With a focus on achievement towards my manuscript revisions. Admittedly, although superficial, I also asked for guidance with my weight loss and finding happiness. Did I want to continue working as a grocery store cashier until I retired? Did I want to remain in Nevada, where memories and the past lingered on every corner? Or was I needing to build roots someplace new, to really start fresh?

"Alright, I'm going to do a brilliant job on my revisions. Editing will come easily for me. I'll know exactly what needs to be cut and what needs to be added. See, already a positive manifestation of attitude. That's all I need to get me over this hump and turn things back around."

I parked the car, grabbed my two bags of groceries, and hurried inside before anyone and their dog came outside. After unloading the bags, I adjusted everything on the desk as though the manifestation energy was going to be critical about my clutter and eased into the chair.

"Water or tea? I need tea." I sprang up and hurried to make myself a cup, knowing the afternoon was already getting away from me.

With the steaming mug of tea on the coaster to my right, I prepared for a surge of positive energy to vibrate through my fingers into my purple editing pen.

"Cake. I need my birthday cake."

Thankfully, I'd nabbed the last nine-inch round chocolate cake. They were out of single slices, not counting vanilla cake, of which they had a ton. And undoubtedly so because vanilla doesn't say *party* or *celebrate*, it said *relax, unwind, don't go crazy.*

I sliced a Winnie the Pooh-size piece, after all, charity begins at home, and grabbed a fork.

"Okay, no more excuses." The tea was still steaming as the slice of cake sat on my left and my manuscript was in the center. "Oh, music, I need mood-setting concentration music."

I turned on the TV and located YouTube, finding a classical playlist because I couldn't focus to songs with lyrics. I became too distracted and sang along.

"Okay, now I'm ready."

```
I watch for his shadow against the
 hall wall. Presentation is every-
thing. A smile, not too happy, but not
suspicious. Warm, slightly unperfect
           always wins.
```

Knock, knock, knock.

"You've got to be kidding me."

When I opened the door, Todd was there with a goofy grin on his face. But my face held fast to its disgruntled frown.

"Ouch, what's up with you?" Todd asked.

"Just trying to edit."

"Sorry, but I wanted to see if you had plans right now."

"I do, I'm supposed to be editing." I checked my fitness watch. "Technically, I should have been editing for the last two hours."

"But it's your birthday." Todd's smile faded.

"Does everyone around here group text?"

"Sometimes. So, can you break away?"

"I really can't."

"Okay." He turned and headed away. "Best of luck with the editing."

I slowly closed the door, feeling horrible. But I had to put my foot down or the first round of edits would never be finished, let alone a publishable manuscript. I returned to the chair.

```
This is the life I needed, but not the
  one I wanted. Yet, I'm not sure how
       much longer I can go on.
```

"Crap." I pictured Todd's face, the sadness that creased over it when I shot him down.

"No, I must edit."

I wiggled in my seat, commanding myself to get back into the mind of my character August.

It's my birthday . . .

I shook my head. "I'm never going to get this story done."

I grabbed my jacket, leaving the cake and tea to fend for themselves, and headed out the front door.

I reached Todd's condo and knocked. He opened it quicker than I expected, and it caused me to stumble back.

I peered around him, checking for the ferocious Whidbey, but there was nothing.

"Hey, sorry about a few minutes ago. What did you have in mind?"

He grinned. "There is an art gallery one town over, right along the beach. They have blown glass, watercolors, and a bunch of artsy stuff. I thought it might be fun to go. Maybe something will help spark some more editing creativity. And you can work on your pet-rified issue."

"It's not an issue. And thanks, but no thanks. You lost me at Whidbey."

He grabbed my hand as I spun around. "But I had you at artsy."

"I'd really like that idea, minus Sir Jumps a Lot."

Todd leaned out the door. "He can hear you and doesn't like the nickname."

"He earned it."

"Can you really have a good birthday stuck inside? Alone?"

I glanced back over my shoulder.

"I'll buy you the best fudge brownie you've ever tasted."

"Sir Jumps a Lot better be known as Sir Stays Away."

Todd smirked and turned around, grabbing the leash off the hook by the door.

Chapter 24

The streets were full of white tent canopies that backed up toward the misty shoreline. Even with the gray skies, there were more people out than I'd expected. Back in Nevada, if it looked like this outside, residents would hunker down watching movies. Whidbey was in his correct location: farthest from me on the left side of Todd, while I was on the right, with space to spare. We stepped into the massive cluster of people and headed down the first aisle.

It felt slightly claustrophobic being around so many people. Other than the grocery store, I'd really been holed up inside, and between this and today's bistro lunch, my brain was on stimulation overload. The isolated person I'd grown into caused me to flinch as each stranger brushed past me. The long days behind the desk were slowly getting to me, making me skittish and unapproachable.

"Are you okay?" Todd asked, his hand finding its way to my back.

"Yes, I was just thinking how crowded it is here."

"It's not as bad as other years. More come out when the sun is shining."

"I've been hiding out way too much." I stepped closer to Todd as though he were safe and could protect me from the anxiety that was stirring inside.

"I told you that a month ago," Todd stated, like a parent of a troubled teenager.

"It's not my fault. How else do you write if you don't sit behind a desk?"

"You can get that talking thing. It dictates for you."

I glanced over at him and squinted. "Last I checked, my bank account doesn't have the budget for that."

"You could have been less weird from the start and used a laptop."

"I'm not being weird. I went old school. People find it charming. The internet is too distracting, and apparently so are everyday things, like art fairs." I motioned around, because we both knew I should be home editing.

"You can turn off the internet. Or, I don't know, have self-control. Besides, can you reach the internet down there?"

"Wow." I halted. "At least I don't get hit in the head by the satellites orbiting Earth."

He noticed I was no longer next to him and stopped. "I get it, I do, I'm joking. But I'm not a writer. I'm someone who has bad knees and a bad back from climbing on roofs all day."

"Well, think about how distracted you get by the news, your son, your list of errands, dating. Try muting those. I've learned it's a challenge."

"I don't doubt it, but I didn't know you were dating."

"I'm not dating, but I'm sure you are, among other things you do."

Todd side-eyed me. "It seems the women I want to date don't want to date. Look, I want you to succeed, but I don't want you to turn into a recluse. There must be a happy medium."

"You think I'm a recluse?" I felt my forehead creasing between my eyebrows.

"Not entirely."

I pouted. "I have a lot on my plate mentally, but I'm working on it." I couldn't help thinking about his response to dating as I moved toward a display of pottery, dog bowls, mugs, salad bowls, and vases. "Lovely," I said to the woman behind the table.

"Thank you. Is there anything in particular you're looking for?" the potter asked.

"The secret to no distractions," Todd said over my shoulder.

I turned back to him and gave him a look of not being amused. "Tell the entire world why don't you."

"I told her, not the world." Todd scratched his chin dramatically. "She's a writer. She'll never have enough coffee mugs."

He and Whidbey were getting too close for my comfort, so I stepped sideways.

I shook my head. "No, I don't need anything but thank you."

"My T-R-E-A-T." Todd glanced at Whidbey and then fished out cash from his wallet, counting it as he went. "And I'll also take a dog bowl. The blue one is nice."

"Well, thank you." I blushed.

"May the mug and its future contents bring you caffeinated, distraction-free productivity." The potter winked at me.

"I sure hope so."

We watched as she wrapped the bowl and mug in thick ocean-blue tissue paper and slid them into a handled bag.

"Thank you." Todd took the bag and carried on down the path, slowing at each booth to take in the sea of blown glass, acrylic paintings, and wood carvings. It was inspiring to see the various skill sets of these artists and also in a way debilitating. How easy it must be to craft a known something, like a mug, where all you had to worry about was what colors would look good together. Or a painting, where you could just paint what you saw in front of you. For a story I had to create a world out of nothing. Pulling bits and pieces of real-world places together to make it feel authentic. Not that I was writing science fiction, but I needed to create a realistic fictional place. World-building. I had to create characters that were perfect enough to cheer for but also not too perfect that they weren't realistic. I instantly aspired to be a painter or sculpture, anyone that could be creative with less pressure. Heck, I could be a florist.

"Analena?" Todd interrupted my thoughts.

"Just daydreaming about those more fortunate with their creativity." I bumped my shoulder against him.

"You must stop thinking about what others are doing and focus on what you need to do."

"And what gives you the authority to say this to me?" I stopped walking.

"Just trying to help."

"Well, your help is coming off as slightly pushy." I crossed my arms.

Todd tilted his head. "That's not what I'm trying to do. And I apologize."

"I'd like to see you write a story."

"I'd like to see you love animals."

"Right." I sighed and glanced at Whidbey.

"What is the major hurdle your facing?"

"I only get to pick one?" I weaved through the crowd to keep from getting too close to Whidbey as we continued down the path. "I fear I'm writing crap, and it's as though what I write can't be erased. That I can't go back and change it because I'm talentless."

"That's because it can't. You used a typewriter." Todd smirked. "But you can once you get it into an electronic doc."

"Ha. Ha." We made our way out of the crowds and further down the beach, and I pulled out my cell and snapped a picture of the tents to post on social media later. "I created a minor problem for myself. But I'm working on getting it all into a Word doc. I guess a part of me is afraid to type it up. Maybe I'm afraid of success because I don't feel I deserve it."

"That's ridiculous. You deserve whatever you desire. The question is what do you want to gain from writing a novel? Why did you make it a life goal?"

"I want to be something other than just a cashier, just an ex-wife. It's my Rubicon."

"I knew you were a Jeep girl!" Todd raised his free hand up in a high-five motion.

"Not that kind." I glanced at his hand as he lowered it.

"I'm aware. I was just having fun." He gestured with his hand. "Continue."

"As a childless woman, I think there are times— No, I know there are times when I question if I'm really a woman, if I'm giving something back to the world by leaving something good behind. I'm the only one I know in my circle of friends, family, and coworkers who doesn't have children. There is a sense of failure in being childless, even if it's by choice. I want to have something substantial and meaningful to show for my life."

"But what about Piepie? Is her life meaningless?"

I grabbed his arm. "You're right. She and Frank don't have kids. She matters so much to so many, and she's made the world a better place. I guess because she always makes it seem like her pets are her kids, I sort of forgot." I gasped. "Does this mean I have to get a pet to leave a mark in this world?"

"Sounds plausible to me." Todd pointed to a bench flanked by azure-blue pots brimming with lemongrass. "And this story you're writing will help you achieve that goal?"

"I don't know. It might all be for nothing. It might be a complete waste of time. I hope it's not. I hope that I'm not here on earth for no reason, no purpose."

"I don't think you are. You have a purpose, even if it's not obvious to you yet." Todd sat down on the bench, keeping Whidbey on the left side. "And is your thriller novel going to bring good to the world?"

"Well, no, but maybe a reader is having a bad day or is sick in the hospital, and my story will help them escape. I'm not saying that I'll be the next James Patterson or anything, but I must hope that I can be something worthy, someone that matters."

"But you are."

A lump formed in my throat. "I'm nobody."

"You're someone to me." Todd grabbed my hand and clenched it.

I was completely thrown off guard and watched him as though in slow motion. I looked at his hand wrapped around mine and shivered. Warmth was growing inside of me like a fire. I didn't know what to say to Todd. Sure, he was handsome and nice, but he had a dog and a son. I had a life to go back to in Nevada. This year was about writing my novel, not about finding love. I'd already proven I'd failed at that with Dawson. Maybe Todd just meant it as a friend. Friends can mean something, something important. Yes, friends. "Thank you, Todd. You mean something to me too."

Then Todd kissed me, and it happened so fast I couldn't stop it, and when his warm lips pressed against my cold ones, I melted into him, leaning my body closer. My eyes fluttered even under my closed eyelids. I couldn't help but think about Dawson kissing me. The thought flashed in my mind—although powerful, this was different. Todd kissing me felt special, deep, and meaningful as the sensation traveled through my body. He wrapped me in his arms, and I pressed myself into him. Our kiss was anything but friendly. That was passion, and another distraction I couldn't afford.

Chapter 25

It had been exactly two days since Todd had kissed me at the art walk. Obviously, I knew how I felt about him, just not how I felt about a relationship with him, as I couldn't let my mind go there. So, I'd been avoiding him. And just because I was avoiding him didn't mean I wasn't thinking about him constantly. My brain was Todd central, and I needed to Zen out so I could refocus on finishing up my manuscript transfer from paper to a Word document.

I pulled up YouTube and searched for yoga by voicing it into the remote, which the system heard as *toga*.

I pressed the button again on the remote and enunciated, "YO-GA."

This time it understood and populated multiple yoga videos. Laying out a blanket as a mat, I lit a candle and changed out of my pajamas and into yoga pants and a T-shirt. Pressing play, the video rolled through greenery followed by pink and purple shades until it came to a twentysomething beanpole of a woman in stretchy pants and a halter tank top. Her abs were flat enough that you could balance a water bottle on them.

I prepared myself and sat, crossing my legs, my belly rolls enough to engulf a water bottle. Following her prompts, I glided through each move. Child's pose, triangle pose, tree pose with deep breaths in, out, and moving into the downward dog. But my hands were sweaty, and my right one slipped forward an inch, and that was when I heard a Velcro-ripping sound followed by pain radiating from my right shoulder. I dropped to my knees and froze, looking like a human table.

"Oh no, what was that?" I held my shoulder, my heartbeat racing. "What have I done?"

I sat back on my heels and closed my eyes. Fear raced through my limbs to my ears, filling them with the *thump, thump, thump* of my heartbeat. The fact that I'm alone hit me. Every bad decision I've made up to this point in my life suddenly came crashing down on me. What had I been thinking moving here and renting a white-on-white condo? What business did I have getting divorced so that I'm alone and helpless? Why did I believe I could write a novel? Whatever happened to my shoulder would never have occurred if I'd not allowed myself to get heavy and then think I could lose weight by doing yoga. Why couldn't I finally let enough be enough? Let the fat rolls roll. Freaking perimenopause. *I want to be twenty again!*

"It's going to be okay. It *must* be okay." I took a deep breath and raised my arm. Pain shot through the right one as I kept my left hand on it as though it would help. With shaky legs, I stood and made my way to the front door, swiping my purse off the hook as I went.

"Hey, Analena!" Todd called as I stepped outside.

I went to lock the front door and realized I couldn't lift my right arm up high enough to put the key in the lock. "You've got to be kidding me." I attempted to lock it with my left hand, but I'm right-handed and dropped the keys on the welcome mat. Even reaching down hurt my shoulder. I fight to hold in curse words that appear like angry red balloons in my mind.

"Analena?"

I turned around as quickly as I could. My face scrunched up as the sun was directly overhead and intensely bright. "Sunglasses. Crap." I'm not going back inside, so I'll have to go without. "Todd. Hey."

"Are you alright? Why are you holding your arm like that?" He pointed.

Thankfully, I didn't see Whidbey because I would have no way of fending off the beast in my current state. "I don't know." I stepped onto the parking lot.

"You don't know why you're holding your arm?"

"I know why I'm holding my arm like this. I don't know what I did to it. To my shoulder."

He shuffled behind me like a puppy, eager for attention. "What did you do?"

I paused at the driver's side door. "I was doing yoga and heard what sounded like Velcro ripping, and now it is throbbing all up and down my arm."

Todd reached around me and took the keys from my hand. "Let me drive. Are you going to the doctor?"

I glanced at my keys and then up at Todd. "I don't know. I don't even know where one is. Maybe I need a hospital." Tears welled up.

Todd moved and stood directly in front of me. "Where does it hurt?"

"Top of my shoulder, but sort of runs down to my elbow and around my bicep."

"Can you move your arm? How's your range of motion?"

"I'm too afraid to move it."

"May I?" He reached out and took hold of my arm. "I've had some pretty nasty accidents with all my roofing jobs." He slowly moved my arm up, then he placed one hand on top of my shoulder. "It doesn't feel warm. And it's not swollen."

"That's good?"

He broke into a smile. "Yes. Your range of motion seems off. You make faces when you're in pain."

"I do?"

Todd nodded.

"Does that mean surgery? What does it mean?"

"If you needed surgery, you would know. I once tore the muscle right off the bone so badly that I had to put my hand in my pocket to keep my arm from swinging all over the place like a rag doll."

"That's . . . terrifying." My mouth gaped open. "Why would you tell me that?"

"To let you know you're not dying because your face makes it look like you are. You have insurance, right?"

I shook my head. "I don't know who will take it since it's out of state. The dentist wouldn't."

"Let's take your car. You can't climb into my truck like that. We'll see what we can find out on the way there about the insurance." He walked around to the passenger side of the Toyota and opened the door for me. I eased in, careful not to bump my arm on anything. Then Todd secured my seat belt, and even though he had sawdust and grimy work clothes on, he smelled like aspen and mint when he leaned over me. And I suddenly forgot about nearly everything and started worrying about whether I'd ever be able to wrap my arms around him again.

It turned out, according to the handy-dandy internet, going to the hospital would have been a waste of time and money. I needed to see an orthopedic specialist, and Ocean Cove didn't have one, so Todd drove me to Crooked River, and thankfully, the only orthopedic doctor accepted my insurance and had an opening. Todd waited in the lobby when I was taken back to see the doctor. The anxiety was building inside me, and I was full-on ugly crying by the time Dr. Cebert walked in.

"I'm so sorry. I'm just scared. I've never had anything like this happen before. I mean, I use my shoulder for basically everything." I leaned forward. "I mean, I'm right-handed and a divorcée. How will I get help?"

The doctor gave me a quizzical look and leaned forward. "Don't worry, lots of people are divorced."

I made a dumbfounded face.

"Do you have a history of any injuries to your right shoulder? Anything that you did prior to the injury today?" Dr. Cebert sat on the padded stool and rested his ankle on his opposite knee.

"Well, around Christmastime I threw my typewriter. My shoulder was sore for a few days."

"You threw a typewriter?" He looked perplexed, but not enough to ask why I'd thrown it.

I nodded. "Not my proudest moment."

"I should think not." The doctor motioned for me to stand. "I'm going to do some range of motion tests."

Dr. Cebert had me push back on his arms as we went through awkward types of pushing and pulling tests. He stopped between each one and scribbled down notes on a scrap piece of paper. An actual scrap, like he tore a piece off to write his grocery list on it. The fact that he wasn't using a laptop made me very concerned that somebody else was going to have to decipher his penmanship. I've seen documentaries where a patient goes in for a gallbladder removal and they amputate a leg instead.

"Do you think I'll need surgery?" My voice was shaky.

"I'll order an MRI and some X-rays. Once we get the results, then we can come up with a plan of action."

"Can you give me any idea of what's going on? Do you think surgery will be needed? I tend to be a self-researcher and like to get ahead of the problem if possible."

"Ah, a Google medical doctor. I love those." His face was stern.

"Research is a good thing. My best friend had a medical issue, and her doctor pulled up the internet." I blinked. "For the answer . . . a doctor used the internet for an answer."

He nodded as though I was lying.

"Anyway, when you go in with knowledge, you're better able to handle change."

He shook his head after a long pause. "In order to help your *research*, it looks like you possibly have a rotator cuff tear, a SLAP tear, or frozen shoulder. The extent of damage is unknown until we get some test results in. Although frozen shoulder wouldn't make that Velcro noise you heard." He looked at the form I had filled out in the lobby. "Happy belated birthday. I see you turned forty."

I eyed him suspiciously. "Yes."

"These types of injuries can be common in women going through . . . certain phases in life. Let me guess, you were lifting heavy weights because you saw it trending online."

"No, I don't even have weights to lift. Well, the gym does, but I have yet to lift over five-pound weights."

"What about a weighted vest, picked it up wrong?"

I shook my head. "If you're asking if I'm doing any of the menopause exercise recommendations all over social media, I'm not. I was doing yoga. Downward dog, and what are the odds since I don't like dogs."

"You don't like dogs?"

"I feel that this is a punishment. The not liking dogs and I injure myself in a yoga hold with the word *dog* in it."

"Does seem a little Alanis Morissette-style ironic." He half laughed. "Alright, I just want you to know that you're not alone. There are lots of women at this stage of their lives. I hope that brings some comfort."

"It does not. Besides, my focus is on the deadline for my novel. Will I be able to type?"

"Depends on how much you like pain." He chuckled, and then he looked at me and saw I was not laughing. "Not in the mood for jokes, okay." Dr. Cebert jotted down something on his piece of paper.

"Is there a way to get the needed testing done today? I'm actually staying over in Ocean Cove, and this was a bit of a drive."

"Sure, on your way out, check with Lauren and she'll try to get you squeezed in." Dr. Cebert stood up and reached for the knob, then turned around. "Try to take it easy until we get a plan in place. You don't want to do any further damage."

I sat in the room and allowed several minutes to pass. A part of me couldn't stop feeling sorry for myself and questioning why such a thing had happened. Not that this was a life-threatening injury, but it was taking away the everyday mobility and functionality that I depended on as a single woman and now as a writer. I needed to remind myself that no matter what the outcome was that I would get through it. Because at that exact moment, I didn't feel like I was going to get through it. How was I to find the mental fortitude I needed? I didn't have enough of it to go around before. In that moment, I stood and made my way to the lobby, stopping halfway to wipe my tears. Everything I'd ever thought of as far as God, the universe, fate, luck . . . now seemed lost.

Chapter 26

Spring

Spring comes much later in the Pacific Northwest, or so I discovered. And people were even joyous about it. Everything seemed to be blooming to its full extent in Ocean Cove. The tulips, hyacinths, and daffodils were showing off their purples, pinks, and yellows. The apple and cherry trees were full of muted pink and snowy white flowers. Yet I couldn't help feeling sad because while everything around me was bursting with color, bringing forth hope and life, I felt the complete opposite. I wanted nothing more than to enjoy it, but instead I was wrapped up in an isolated thunderstorm of grumpiness.

I'd instantly discovered that my shoulder was in charge of everything I do daily, from rolling over in bed, to sitting up, to reaching for a glass from the cupboard. Don't even get me started on the challenge of changing clothes and showering. The MRI results were taking longer than the three days the doctor had promised. And I'd spent those days in my pajamas, barely leaving the couch. My hermit status had become ultra-hermit because of this stupid shoulder and radiating arm pain. The only thing that got me out of the condo was the follow-up appointment a week later.

"Analena," Dr. Cebert said as he walked into the room, "let's go over those results."

I didn't want to tell him that my shoulder hurt a lot worse than when the injury occurred. I'd already skirted around Todd offering to drive me all the way back out to Crooked River by saying it was feeling better.

Dr. Cebert pulled out a chair at the desk and clicked around with the mouse, loading the computer screens with images of my shoulder. "Alright, let's start with your X-rays. See this here?" He pointed at the image. "This all looks good as far as the bone goes. I see a little bit of arthritis, but nothing to be concerned about. It's not causing the pain that you have or the limited range of motion." He clicked around and loaded another screen. "This is where my concern lies. In your MRI. If you look right here, this area should be smooth, and it is not. This is where your rotator cuff tear is visible. Now, if you have frozen shoulder, that won't show up on here."

"So, surgery?" My bottom lip quivered.

"It's possible. Most of my patients respond well to physical therapy and an injection to help with the inflammation. It all depends on what you're willing to do and how your body responds."

Honestly, everything that I'd seen in my online research was that this doctor was going to push for surgery without any other options, so I was sort of fumbling through my thoughts, leaving me a bit confused. I thought I would need to put up more of a fight on the nonsurgical option. "What are we talking about as far as recovery time goes without surgery? Because I have a deadline I must meet, and I need to be able to type."

"The recovery process can take anywhere between six months to a year going the non-surgical route. But even with surgery, you would be looking at a pretty significant recovery time as well. Either way you'll need physical therapy. There are many advances that you can use to help you write, such as dictation. You can look into getting some help around the house so that you can give it proper time to heal. You need to limit things you do such as cooking and cleaning and lifting anything away from your body. You need to be careful with your basics, too—showering, dressing."

I couldn't tell him I had zero help at home; he couldn't fix that. I would just have to figure out how to get by on my own. "How much is this all going to cost? I have insurance, but it doesn't cover everything."

"Your insurance company can handle that information. Everyone's is different. But there is a good physical therapy place here in Crooked River. Come back in six weeks and we'll see how everything is progressing and can go from there."

"Are you hinting that this is all going to work out?"

"What did your Google doctor tell you?"

I tried not to laugh. "To ask my doctor."

"Hmm, well, surgery is always a possibility, just like rainbows and hope." He stood up. "Make sure you keep your focus on the latter."

I grabbed my purse with concentrated effort to do it with my nondominant hand.

Dr. Cebert stopped as he reached for the door handle. "I have faith that you'll overcome this. In fact, this is little, and yes, if you saw what I see in my line of work, it is a minor injury. A little setback. Although it doesn't feel like it right now. It's a slight bump on life's road. It's my belief that things are not laid in your path that you can't get through. Even if you don't have hope now, you will. You just have to get through this in order to stay on your path." Dr. Cebert smiled and exited into the hall.

I stopped and thought about his words right there in the middle of the empty exam room. And as I walked towards the reception desk, I thought about what the doctor had said. Maybe the only way to get through something was to actually go through it, no matter the level of pain.

Chapter 27

I stared at the stack of typed words on the paper and back at my tablet with attached mini keyboard. "This is starting to seem like a very ridiculous idea. I really should've used a laptop from the start. What was I thinking, Jessica Fletcher?"

I've spent the last two days drowning in self-pity and ice cream when I should've been typing the final section of my manuscript into the Word document. Not that I could do it well, but I had one good working hand.

With all the co-pays and deductibles for my shoulder injury, not to mention the bill for my dental work, I didn't have the funds to cover any type of dictation program that actually worked. And I had yet to find out if the dictation in Word was worth a darn because I simply couldn't bother to try.

I sat on the patio chair I'd dragged in all those months ago so I could sit at the desk, one handed, and decided that I wouldn't be moving it back out no matter how nice a day it was outside. The patio chair was inside and was here to stay.

A knock at the door caused me to glance down at what I was wearing. Pajamas with this morning's strawberry jelly stain in the middle of my top. My hair was unwashed because I needed both hands to give it a proper scrub. I've been putting off washing it until I had to go to my first PT session tomorrow. I didn't need to be presentable until then.

I pulled open the door, wedged myself between it and the wall. "Hey, Todd." Instantly I regretted the whole non-washed hair thing.

He looked awake, refreshed, and cheery. "Good morning. I brought breakfast." He held up a sandwich-sized paper bag.

"I already ate but thank you."

"Everyone can use a second breakfast from time to time. Helps with your needed protein intake." He wiggled the bag, and it crinkled. "Writing protein."

"I'm not dressed."

"You're not naked."

I glanced down as though I wasn't sure. "Correct." I looked back up at him, his grin very big. "You're not giving up, are you?"

Todd shook his head. I stepped back and opened the door all the way. And that's when I spotted Whidbey. I swung the door closed with my good arm.

"Hey," Todd yelled through the door.

"You have the beast."

"Readers bring dogs to book signings."

I pressed my forehead against the door. "They do." I knew they did. I'd seen them before, especially at nonfiction signings where the author wrote about dogs.

Easing the door open, I stuck my face out. "I don't really think this is a skill I need to develop."

"He'll be a perfect gentleman. I'll make him lie down, and he won't invade your space. You don't want to be known as the author who hates dogs."

"I don't hate dogs. I just don't like them near me." I thought about how that sounded and knew I'd lost this fight. "Fine, but he better behave."

Stepping back, I hid behind the door as Todd and Whidbey entered. He set the breakfast bag on the kitchen counter and instructed the dog to lie down in front of the unlit fireplace. "I'm here to be your hands. Laundry, dishes, and typing."

I leaned against the counter, eyeing the bag with an even sharper eye on Whidbey. "No, you don't have to do that."

"I don't, but I want to." Todd opened the bag and peered into it. "Sprinkles or glazed?"

"Depends, rainbow sprinkles or chocolate?"

"All sprinkles are the same."

"Excuse me, not even close. There is a taste difference."

"Okay then, close your eyes. You tell me if this is rainbow or chocolate." He grabbed a napkin and reached into the bag.

I rested my left hand on the counter and closed my eyes. I heard the bag rustle and sensed his presence in front of me. I could smell the aspen and mint again. *Could he at least smell bad once in a while?*

"Open up," Todd said, his voice even closer now.

He gently placed the doughnut on my bottom lip as I took a bite. I allowed the sugary goodness to rest on my tongue for a few seconds. I pressed my lips together, then said, "Chocolate."

Todd snickered, and I opened my eyes.

"Ahh, I was right." I pumped my left fist into the air.

"Shocking." He set the rest of the donut on the napkin next to me. "I hope you like chocolate over rainbow."

I smiled and picked up the doughnut. "I do."

Todd removed a glazed donut from the bag and held it up. "I need energy to type."

"No, honestly, I can't have you do that. You would be typing for a long time."

"I'd like to be here for a long time. Dylan is with his mom, and I don't have work today."

"What about Whidbey? He can't be happy inside all day?"

"He's having a spa day. I'll have to run out and drop him off soon."

"Spa day?"

"You know, N-A-I-L trim, B-A-T-H."

"Ahh a—"

Todd's index finger found my lips. "If you didn't learn from T-R-E-A-T, then you will most certainly learn now."

I nodded and took another bite of the chocolate-sprinkled doughnut. "How will I repay the favor with one good shoulder?"

"Be my date for this work thing next weekend."

I choked on the doughnut. "That seems like an unfair trade."

"You haven't been to my work functions. Trust me, it's like a family reunion with all your exes."

"So, why do you go?"

"Because I like to keep myself employed."

"That much drama in construction work?"

"Oddly enough, yes."

I took another bite of doughnut. The chocolate sprinkles stuck to my upper lip. "I would be happy to go with you to the work function. You don't have to help me type in return."

"I want to." Todd finished his glazed and rinsed his hands in the sink. "Let's get this story transfer finished up. There can't be too much left."

"There isn't." We headed toward the desk; I shimmed as close to the kitchen as possible so that I could keep my distance from Whidbey, who raised his head as I passed. I pressed my finger onto the tablet, allowing it to unlock. Todd pulled the patio chair out. I took the stack of remaining pages and adjusted myself on the couch nearby and watched. Which felt odd, but what else was I going to do. Beside I needed to rest my arm. But I soon found myself trying not to snicker. *I thought my typing skills were bad*. I'd never seen anyone examine each key before pecking at it.

"What does *QWERTY* mean to you?" I asked, stifling a laugh.

"Not sure, is that half a quart in German?"

I stood up and leaned over his shoulder, glancing at the screen. "Does that say she grabbed a bun? No, it should be 'she grabbed a gun.'"

"The *g* is on top of *b*. You're the one with the dinky little keyboard. Maybe it's a baking mystery?"

I slumped back onto the coffee table. "It's not a cozy mystery."

"What draft is this?"

"Technically, this will be the third. I sort of line-edited the first draft as I went. My shoulder injury came right during the final leg of typing."

"I'll do my best to get this all keyed in for you."

"And I'll try not to be a grump."

"You, grumpy? Never."

"Very funny. I've been grumpy since I tore my rotator cuff. It absolutely sucks. I feel so helpless, because I am.

I'm making something that should be easy harder because I was trying to be all Jessica Fletcher."

Emotions bubbled over like pasta water without salt in the pot. My plate felt so full, and my mind and body drained from nothing going the way I planned. I was so wrapped up in my feelings that I didn't notice Whidbey until it was too late.

Warm, furry-like firmness pressed into the top of my knee, and damp wetness pushed at my hand. I couldn't move. I tried to fold into myself and pinched my eyes closed. A low cry-like whimper filled the air.

"Calm down, you're alright." I heard Todd's voice.

Was he talking to me or the dog? The whiny noise continued.

"Analena. You're okay."

I opened my eyes, bringing the room back to life, and then realized the noise was me.

"He's worried about you; he just came over to say hi and try to distract you. He does it with Dylan when his anxiety is high. Whidbey is trying to get you to pet him so that you can redirect your thoughts."

I glanced down. "He's a therapy dog?"

Todd laughed. "Not at all, he sort of just started doing it a few years ago."

Whidbey was sitting at my feet, his heavy chin still pushed into my leg, his nose nudging me. Tremors filled my hand as I lifted it up a few inches, letting it hover over the dog's head. I gave one quick pat, his soft fur almost shocking, and then pulled my hand back.

Todd stood up and patted his leg. "Whidbey, she's not ready for you yet. Come and lie down, back where you were." He pointed to the front of the fireplace. "Good boy."

I took a deep breath as Whidbey obeyed orders. "You mean that wasn't part of your two-pronged plan?"

Todd returned to the chair. "Nope, that was all you. My plan has been more subtle. You haven't even realized it's been occurring."

"Well, I'm sorry about complaining and getting emotional."

"Don't apologize. I've been there. Injuries that made me feel like you'd never get better."

Except for the breaking waves outside the slider and the sounds of seagulls calling out, the room was silent.

"I'm sorry."

"Stop apologizing. Just think about all that you have. I hate to say it, but it seems like you forgot how lucky you are. Taking an entire year off to follow your dream. Not many get that chance. Yes, your injury sucks, but you'll get through it."

"You're right. I really need to work on that. It appears I have a lot of things to work on, and it's not resonating because I feel as lost as when I first arrived here."

Todd turned to me, resting his elbows on his knees. "When has anything ever gone as planned?"

"Well, I got the color of the sprinkles correct." I faked a smile.

He laughed and bowed his head. We seemed so far away when he had been typing, and now he was close. The light from the window slowly crept across the wall of the living room. It rested just over my shoulder, and I could see the beams dancing through my hair. I couldn't help but think about the kiss at the art fair as he gazed into my eyes. His hand moved forward and touched a strand of hair, pushing it behind my ear, causing me to shiver. I hoped he didn't notice.

"You look beautiful, Analena."

I glanced down because I didn't feel beautiful, especially in my stained pajamas. But I'd vowed to do better, even if it felt odd. "Thank you." I smiled.

Todd smiled back, and when he leaned closer, my eyes fluttered shut. Then my mind traveled back to Nevada. Like a slingshot, I was looking at my townhouse, and that caused me to open my eyes. I sucked in my lower lip as I leaned back, away from him.

"I'm leaving in the summer. I don't know what this is, if it's anything." I motioned with my left hand between us. "But it would be a mistake for me to get into a relationship. This wasn't supposed to happen."

Todd kept his hand outstretched, resting on my cheek. "No, it wasn't supposed to happen, but that's what's great about life. The unexpected."

Then he went to his knees, so we were eye level and gently pulled me closer to him. He kissed me as though I was all he'd been thinking about since our last kiss.

Chapter 28

"You need to stop kissing Todd," Amy said.

"I'm *not* kissing him. I'm only *participating*. He kissed me first," I said and ran my hand through my hair, staring at the phone's screen. "Why do I feel like I'm in high school arguing with you all over again?"

"Well, out with it. How was the kiss?"

I could feel Amy's eyes judging me through the phone. She was probably tapping her elbow with her right hand while she crossed her arms over her chest.

"It's more like kisses." I blushed.

"Analena! You said no romance, and you're romancing!"

"We're not romancing, we're friending. Where Todd and I find ourselves currently doesn't matter. I'm leaving in a few months. And I will not be starting a long-distance relationship."

"Friends don't kiss."

"Some do."

"Friends shouldn't kiss romantically. So, I'm assuming it was a friend kiss, no romance behind it?"

I put my finger to my mouth and bit it. "So, how are the girls?"

"Fine, be that way. You're an adult. At least tell me how the writing is going?"

"Sort of like if all the words fell out of all the books in the library and I tried to put them back together into a single book." I sighed. "The shoulder injury has really set me back. But the story is now, finally, all in a Word document."

"Did you use dictation for any of it?"

"I tried the voice thing in Word. It looks like it's trying to transcribe a three-year-old on a sugar high. It lags, then it doesn't do any of the quotation marks and gets at least twenty percent of the words wrong. And I don't have the funds to buy a fancy program that would probably work better. But that's a moot point now. It's all there, I just don't know how well I'll be able to type up edits because I can't dictate those. My entire plan was to have submitted the manuscript to agents and publishers in New York City, with a pretty little bow on it, *before* I headed home. Now, I'm not so sure."

"We talked about this. They don't do that anymore. I think everything is sent via email."

"Yes, it seems like they only want them sent by email. I just kind of like the idea of submitting a manuscript the way it once was instead of trying to figure out if somebody lost it in their digital mailbox."

"Don't worry, they'd just as easily lose it in their snail-mailbox. Besides, if you mail it, they'll probably think you're ninety-five years old."

I can't help but laugh. She's absolutely correct. I've never really been all that flexible with some things.

"So, you have two choices: either live out your spring fling and summer romance with Todd and then disappear back home with a half-heartedly written novel, or laser focus yourself and get it done, without any heart palpitations."

"I hear you, but I feel like I've been going through some type of midlife crisis. It wasn't so apparent when I arrived here, but it's getting worse with each passing day. Not being able to use my arm the way I normally do has been incredibly tiresome and mentally draining. I can't believe how much a shoulder really controls the entire rest of your arm and hand. My hormones are all messed up, too. I've been more emotional than usual. My orthopedic doctor mentioned perimenopause. Which of course I already knew."

"Sounds right, just not sure why an ortho doc would know anything about that." There's a loud scream in the background. "Crap, sorry, I need to go. We'll chat more later. Love you. Make good choices. Bye."

I made my way to the slider, the gentle breeze coming off the breaking waves trickled through the screen door. I cannot believe that I'm feeling sorry for myself, yet again.

I caught my reflection on the open slider, and it was just another reminder that one cannot always see what a person is dealing with. My shoulder looks perfectly fine from the outside, but the air-bubble type of pain radiating down my arm from the top of my shoulder was anything but normal. However, I really did like the thought of spending more time with Todd, although I know it was only going to lead to some form of miniature heartbreak—a fun size candy bar heartbreak, if you will.

I flopped down on the couch, and pain shot through my arm.

"Crap, that hurts." I grabbed at it, wrapping my hand around my bicep because shoulder pain apparently radiates all over the arm.

Washing my hair and dressing had become an embarrassing, deflating, and annoying solo defeat. Taking three minutes to put on a shirt that still caused pain made me feel useless and older than I was. Last night I accidentally rolled over to my right side, and I thought I'd been hit with a two-by-four in the shoulder.

"I need a nice walk. That should help clear my head, fresh sea air on my face." I went to slip on my shoes and realized that I had to position my right shoulder and armpit just right over my knee, but even with that, pain traveled down my arm like lightning. So instead of going for that walk, I kicked off my untied shoes and took a note that I needed to buy a pair of flip-flops. I curled up on the couch and grabbed the TV remote.

There was a knock at my door, and I reluctantly went to answer it. When I pulled it open, Todd was standing there.

He looked me up and down. "You're not ready?"

I tilted my head, questioning what I was to be ready for, then it hit me. "Shoot. Your party!"

It took me twenty minutes to pull on a fancier top and jeans, and doing my hair was out of the question, so I brushed it and put a clip on one side like it was 1993. Thankfully, I could do makeup with one hand and wasn't too big on going super layered, just foundation, powder, mascara, and caramel nude lipstick. I never did eyeshadow because even in the most neutral of colors, it always ended up looking like the blue eyeshadow of Mimi's character from *The Drew Carey Show*.

After exiting Todd's truck, with his help, he didn't let go of my hand. We made our way to the front door of the recreation center where the office party was being held, and I glanced down at our hands.

"We're a couple, remember? We should hold hands," Todd said.

"Right, of course." I didn't want to admit that I loved it but also feared it. So, I kept reminding myself that it was just for the party, even if it gave me all the tingles.

We entered the building, Todd holding the door open for me, and the noise of chatter was overwhelming. There must have been sixty people shoved into the room filled with gray-and-black streamers and matching balloons hanging from the ceiling.

I squeezed Todd's hand. "I didn't expect this many people."

"We have about twenty-five roofers with the company, and they all brought their significant others, plus the boss and his wife. But don't worry, they're all sort of nice." Todd winked.

"Thanks, that doesn't make me feel better."

"Would it help if I introduced you as my long-lost little sister?"

"It would not."

"Good, then it will make us holding hands and kissing less awkward."

"Why would we kiss?"

Todd halted at the edge of one of the round tables decorated with place settings. "Then what are we going to do during spin the bottle?"

I felt my face flush. "You're serious?"

Todd laughed and squeezed my hand. "I'm joking, but the look on your face. You might need a drink."

I beamed a smile. "Now you're talking."

The rest of the party went as I expected. Awkward questions and a lot of help from Todd to cover up our relationship lie. But everyone seemed to buy what he was selling, including me. By the time we were heading back to the truck, I was jealous of our relationship.

"They're really like family, aren't they?" I climbed into the truck with a boost from Todd around my waist and my good elbow. "I think my parents asked fewer questions when I was dating a biker with a neck tattoo when I was twenty-three."

"They care just like family. It's why I enjoy working for the company. But it can make parties unbearable if I come solo. You saw all the spouses in there, without you, I would have been the only single one."

"I wasn't even aware they could pick on you from way up there," I mentioned when he climbed in on the driver's side.

He started up the truck. "I'm surprised no one tripped on you, being way down there."

"Hey, I wasn't the only short one."

Todd smiled and eased onto the main road. "Correct, you were the shortest of the short there."

I smacked his arm.

"Thanks for being my girlfriend. I had a lot of fun."

I bit the side of my lip. "Me too."

We didn't talk the rest of the ride back to the condos as my head was filled with the fact that he never kissed me and I was disappointed about it.

Chapter 29

"Editing with one hand will be easy," I whined sarcastically. "It's official, I give up."

I slammed the tablet closed and eased back into the patio chair. There was a worn spot in the seat cushion, causing the whole thing to sag. It was not meant for eight-hour days of supporting my bum. Out on the sand, in front of the patio, I spotted a woman and a child. For a second, I wondered if it was a nanny and a child. However, as the lady got closer, I noticed that they looked identical. Very Jennifer Garner-and-her-daughter type of identical, and I couldn't help but feel jealous. I'd never get to experience motherhood. I always believed it was a choice I had made, but often I wondered if marrying the wrong man influenced that decision.

I watched the little girl closely inspect something in the sand, pick it up, and then hand the prize to her mother. Together they wandered farther down the shore with the unknown treasure grasped firmly in her mother's hand.

Lately, my manuscript was feeling more like a wandering child and less like a dutiful parent trying to locate it and send it on the correct path. The story was all I had to leave behind in this world. The weight of possibly not being able to complete a final, polished draft due to a shoulder injury weighed on me more than I realized. I thought back to the novels that moved me, encouraged me, gave me joy, and brought me to different worlds. Could my story have the same effect for my readers? I reopened the tablet and positioned my left fingers over the small keyboard and continued to slowly and methodically peck away at my edits.

I lost track of time, and the tablet popped up a warning that I had nine percent battery life left. I checked my fitness watch, realizing I had 368 steps for the day and it was already four thirty.

"Shoot," I groaned as I stood on stiff legs.

I must get my steps in, no matter how my shoulder felt. Walking on the beach seemed less jarring than the treadmill. I spent a solid five minutes trying to dress myself and then grabbed my grocery store flip-flops, intending to take them off once I hit the sand.

But once I made it to the sand, I realized it might be a bad idea. Apparently, to move in heavy, dry sand you used your shoulder. I headed closer to the waves, where the sand was compacted, and decided to go south down the beach instead of north, where the crowds of people were thicker.

I had made it about half a mile when a familiar figure and his dog came into view, making their way towards me.

"Hey," Todd said when he finally reached me.

With Whidbey at his side, it was clear they'd gone for a swim as his fur was all wet and Todd's shoes were in his hand. Half of his jeans were wet and sandy.

"What happened there?" I point at his pants.

"Decided to dip my toes in, then a wave had other plans."

I laughed and wrapped my hand around my aching bicep. Whidbey stepped toward me, and I didn't take a step back. Maybe I was tired, but he seemed less scary today, less beastly with his fur all wet and straggly.

"I was hoping I could provide more help for your manuscript." He grinned.

"I've been doing really well on my own." I didn't smile back.

"You have?"

"As well as a caffeinated woodpecker can edit."

"Sounds interesting." Todd started to walk forward, and I moved to his left side, heading back toward the condos. "Are you possibly free tonight? I was thinking maybe I could cook dinner for you?"

The sunshine was still above the tops of the evergreen trees in the distance. It would be nice not to have to make dinner, but spending time with Todd only made me want him more. Plus, relying on him would make it worse in the long run, especially if I was still injured when I returned home to Nevada. A breeze came off the water, taking Todd's scent with it, tickling my nose and warming my heart.

"That would be nice." *Way to use self-control, Analena.* "Apparently cooking, like everything else, involves using your shoulder, and it's been rather painful to get things out of the fridge, let alone chop up food."

"Wonderful, let me get cleaned up and at least start a little bit of the cooking, and then you can come on over? Or if you would like, I could bring it to your place?"

"I have no problem coming over if Whidbey keeps his distance. I don't want you schlepping around a bunch of dishes."

Todd pulled the cell phone from his pocket and glanced at it. "How does seven thirty work?"

"That works perfectly." I smiled. "I'm going to walk a bit more. Unless you want to wear my watch and help me hit my step goal?"

Todd snorted a laugh. "It's against my principles to partake in a fitness watch cheat scheme. Plus, I don't look good with two watches on. It's a fashion no-no."

I laughed. *Todd looks good in everything.* "See you soon." I gave a wave as I headed down the shoreline, trying my best not to glance back at him or see if he was looking back at me.

Getting changed into a different outfit, because I needed to be a bit fancier for dinner, took longer than normal. It included several awkward faces I caught myself making in the bathroom mirror, and I couldn't help but laugh. I wasn't twenty anymore, so a bra was a must, but it was the most challenging with my injury. To be fair, bras have been challenging since the beginning of time.

I adjusted the tank top on my shoulders, covering up the bra straps, and checked my bat wings that should be hidden in a dark box. A sweater would be ideal, but that would be an impossible feat with my current range of motion. Thankfully, my arms won't do a lot of waving, so I should be okay. I run my left hand through my hair, giving it a tussle; the wavy strands from all the humidity lift it a bit.

At the front door, I slipped on my flip-flops. I have very high arches, so they're not the best, but my feet better get used to it because putting on tennis shoes was problematic and saved for PT days. After doing a final check in the mirror, I headed upstairs to Todd's door and knocked.

What I wasn't expecting was Whidbey to open the door. Okay, he couldn't actually open the door, but it looked real enough to me that I stumbled backwards, tripping over my flip-flops.

"I thought I said no dogs." I held my bad arm.

Todd's head popped from around the door frame. "Dogs? No, Whidbey is only one dog. Are you having double vision?"

"Todd! You said he'd be far away," I said through clenched teeth.

"Far away is not no dogs." He grabbed hold of Whidbey's collar. "Now that you mention it, how great it would be to have two dogs."

"You would." I shimmied past the two of them and into Todd's condo.

I made my way to his couch, knowing the pain in my shoulder lessened when I was resting and my arm wasn't hanging by my side. His couch had a slight dusting of German shepherd hair, and I tucked my feet under my bottom, sitting down. The dog eyed me from his spot next to Todd as he grabbed two wineglasses and brought them toward me. It's not lost on me that while I feared the beast, I was willing to try to squelch my fear to spend time with Todd.

I took the wineglass in my left hand, even though it's awkward since I'm right-handed. Having to remind myself to use my nondominant hand remained a constant memory challenge.

The couch cushions compressed as Todd sat next to me. He was in that perfect spot of too close but not close enough, and it caused my heart to beat faster than normal, and my cheeks turned rosy even before I'd had a sip of wine.

"Sorry, dinner is not quite ready. I figured it would be okay if we sat and talked while I finish cooking," Todd said.

I glanced down into my wineglass and then back up at him and laughed. "It's not like I can do much else with this injured shoulder."

"There are lots of things you can do."

"Like what exactly? I'm not trying to be negative. I'm being realistic. What exactly is it I can do right now other than one-handed keyboard pecking?"

"For starters, you could take up photography. Phone cameras have lots of special features these days, and you only need one hand to use them. You could puzzle. Or play board games; those are fun. How about solitaire? I think I have a deck of cards around here someplace." Todd glanced over his shoulder as though there was a giant deck of cards behind him.

"Those sound great, but puzzles cost money—"

"We have an entire stack of them at the community center, in the cabinets under the books."

"I didn't know that." I glanced down. "I can never remember if it's eight or seven cards that you're supposed to lay out for solitaire. My grandpa was great at it. He had all these different rules that really helped him to create fun games. I just wish I remembered some of them now."

"I promise you it'll get better even if it doesn't seem like that at the moment."

I half-laughed. "I'm wallowing in this woe is me. It's not like I have some horrible disease or am missing an appendage. Just not being able to use my arm like I used to is debilitating mentally." I took a sip of wine. "I feel like all we do is talk about me. Let's talk about you."

"My life is not exciting. Unless you want to talk about Whidbey, or dogs in general, because I could go on for hours about that."

I buried my nose in my wineglass, and Todd laughed.

"How are you doing with your edits?" Todd asks.

"Well, thanks to my fabulous desk and my least-favorite desk chair, it's going about as well as I expect it to."

"*That's* a good thing."

"Okay, Martha Stewart."

Todd smirked as the timer on the oven chirped. "I have never been this excited for anybody to try anything I've ever made before. He jumped up off the couch and headed to the kitchen.

"Should I be fearful that you're going to poison me?"

Todd opened the oven door and glanced over at me from the corner of his eye as he lifted the dish from the oven. "Not intentionally." He slid the dish onto the stovetop as steam rose off it. Whidbey, who had been asleep on his bed, lifted his head, nose twitching. "But at least we'll both go out together—Romeo and Juliet style."

I hesitantly stood and made my way over to the kitchen peninsula with my wineglass while monitoring Whidbey. "I'm not one to die for the love of my life, but it smells good."

"Well, that's a disappointment. Not a die-hard love fan?" Todd yanked off the oven mitts and tossed them on the counter next to the dish.

I think about Dawson. "I'm not a die-hard anything."

"Baked ratatouille with goat cheese." Todd gestured with his whole right hand at the dish and then to the foil next to the two empty plates. "And of course, garlic bread."

"I feel like this is the point when we say something about our wine pairing goes well with this, but I'm not that type of connoisseur. I'm more of an 'Oh look, that bottle is on sale' type of girl."

Todd stuck a spatula into the dish, releasing a puff of steam. "The wine you're enjoying tonight is Côtes du Rhône."

I observed my glass. "I've never had it before. It tastes like ripened peaches and smells like fresh-cut roses."

Todd grabbed the bottle off the counter and spun it around to read the back of the label. "It says it has hints of rose, peach, and vanilla. I think you're more of a connoisseur than you realize."

"Can I ask you a tough question?" I sighed.

"I'm not the best at answering difficult questions but I'll try." Todd served our plates and headed towards the kitchen table, setting them down and pulling out a chair for me. I slid in and set my wineglass to the left of my plate. The dog took up a spot next to Todd, and I noticed I didn't flinch when he was making his move.

As Todd pulled out his own chair and sat down, I watched him as though I'd never seen a man sit before. *Must he exude handsomeness with everything he does?*

"What's it like being a dad? And I mean it in the sense of what it's like being a parent?" It's something I'll never experience, and I honestly hope you say it's horrible and then we talk about the weather."

Todd used the side of his fork to cut a square bite from his plate but didn't bring it to his lips. "It's scary, fun, heartbreaking, challenging, joyful, and exhausting. I think that because my son has autism, I'm not the typical parent to ask. But nowadays, because so many more kids have that diagnosis, maybe there's not as few of us as we think. Being a parent for the first time is unfamiliar. I'd assume that being a parent for the second time is unfamiliar because every child is different. But in the end, we're all still parents, and we love our children, and they still drive us bonkers from time to time."

"I just always have this little pit in my stomach reminding me I'm not like most women. I'm not a mom. Does that make me less of a woman?"

"I don't think it makes you less of anything. You just don't have that experience or set of skills. But it's not to say that at some point you won't get married again and that person might have children or maybe you have a child."

I covered my mouth as I laughed, trying to keep the food from flying all over the table. Once I swallowed, I said, "This body is never having a baby; it's definitely past its best by date."

Todd gave me the side-eye and huffed. "I definitely think you're far from expiration."

I held a slice of garlic bread in front of my face to try to hide how I felt about his comment.

"Look at Piepie and their little family abode of creatures. Everybody has the right to choose what constitutes a family, and as long as there is love and loyalty, that's all that matters. What makes you happy, not others. Let me tell you, if you had a child, you'd quickly realize that everybody is going to judge you and how you parent. It can come from family, friends, even a stranger at the grocery store. Kid or no kid, people judge, so stop judging yourself."

"Let's talk about something more interesting, because that felt rather self-help book like."

"Point taken. So, how's the physical therapy going? I see you're still favoring that arm quite a bit."

I took a bite of the baked ratatouille finally, and it was mouthwatering. My eye lashes fluttered. Who would have thought eggplant could taste unvegetabley. "I'm trying to use it more, move it, because the physical therapist warned me that if I favor it too much, it could get worse for my frozen shoulder, but I have to be careful due to the rotator cuff tear, it's a fine line. When it hurts, like right now, I just kind of feel like my only choice is to stop moving it. Every task is a frustrating and an exhausting ordeal. I mean I actually miss doing laundry, washing dishes, and washing my hair with both hands. You should see me trying to get the laundry from the washing machine into the dryer with one hand. I almost fell into the machine."

"I've seen you walk and trip over air, so I wouldn't put that too far out to pasture. It's possible." Todd laughed, and I reached over and smacked him on the arm. "Ouch."

"That'll teach you."

"Fine, fine."

"Tell me about a book you've read lately?"

"I just finished *Bird by Bird*. Even though I'm not a writer, it sounded good."

"Yes, it's by Anne Lamont."

"You've read it?"

"I have."

"I didn't read anything in it about a writer going old school and manually typing up a manuscript."

"It didn't say not to."

Todd smiled at me.

We finished our meal while discussing our favorite TV shows. Mine was *Prison Break,* and his was a tie between *Arrested Development* and *The Office.* I found myself so lost in conversation that for a moment I completely forgot about my shoulder pain until the final sip of wine was gone from my glass. "Thank you for such a wonderful meal." I set my napkin next to my plate and began to stand.

"Oh, don't think you're going anywhere. I'll take your plate, but we still have dessert."

I eased back into the chair and handed him my plate, which looked like I'd licked it clean. "You really didn't have to make dessert, but I'm not going to turn it down, especially if it's anything like dinner."

"I can't claim dessert." He held his hands up in defense. "I've not done well in the baking department. I picked up a little something from my favorite local bakery."

Todd returned to the table with two small dessert plates and a tan box. He propped open the lid as I leaned forward to peek inside.

"May I present to you, chocolate pecan pie cupcakes." Todd lifted one delicate, frosting-covered item at a time from the box and set them on the plates in front of us.

The cupcake had a parchment wrapping around it, and I peeled it off, simply staring at it for a few seconds, taking in the gooey caramelized pecans sprinkled on top. "It's like a piece of artwork."

"Trust me, you'll get over it quickly once you take a bite. This beauty will disappear like a magic trick."

I noticed that Todd and I both lifted our cupcakes at the same time and put them to our lips. I took a bite, and the caramel pecans tapped the bottom of my nose. When the chocolate hit my tongue, it instantly melted with the gooeyness of the caramel pecans. The only thing that could be better would be a kiss from Todd. I tried to shake off the thought and focused on the cupcake. I'm not here for romance. Frankly, I'm here for this cupcake. "I'm pretty sure I'm gonna need to know the name of this bakery so that I can get two dozen to go."

"The best way to cap off dinner."

After every single last crumb and stickiness was off my dessert plate, I glanced at my watch and realized that our dinner took three hours, and the sun had long disappeared, leaving only the glow of the kitchen light as it danced across the floor into the small dining area.

"Do you have time to stay for a movie?" Todd asked.

"I really wish I could, but my arm is hurting, and I still need to do another round of physical therapy exercises before I get too tired. I'm supposed to do them three to five times a day, and I've only done them once today." I looked at his face, and he actually looked sad, but I know that if I stay, it'll only complicate things.

"Then I'll walk you home, and we can save the movie for another time, say after you've finished your latest round of edits?"

"A celebration movie?"

"I think that's a good way to put it."

Todd and I stood up from the table. That awkward we're standing close, but not too close, and we both looked at each other, then looked away. I couldn't help but feel like a teenager again. Why did love always make you feel so young?

"Whidbey, let's go."

"I thought you said you'd walk me home."

"We're a package deal, extra protection."

I shrugged my good shoulder. "If I'm afraid of him, bad guys should be too."

"Or bad girls."

"Those aren't threats. They're guys' dreams."

Todd huffed as he clipped on the dog's leash. "Not this guy."

If he could stop talking, it would really make it easier not to keep falling for him.

Whidbey shook his head. The tags on his collar jangled together. We made our way out the front door, and I noticed it was another silent evening, not a resident in sight. Even the seagulls seem to have gone to bed. The wind whipped around, and the clouds were thick overhead. It was hard to tell if it was going to rain as, being this close to the beach, it always feels misty and damp.

Todd had one hand on the leash, and the other hand grazed the middle of my back as we made our way to my front door. I unlocked it and then stepped halfway inside, turning back around. Whidbey was sniffing Janet's door, but I still put a door frame between Todd and I, hoping the action would stop me from wanting to kiss him. But as soon as I looked in his eyes, I knew that if he leaned forward, I was going to give in. I've been on that ride before, and I'd buy an annual pass no matter what the price.

"Thank you again for a delightful dinner, interesting conversation, and a divine dessert. I think I'll probably be dreaming about it tonight," I said.

"I'll have some nice dreams tonight, too." Todd glanced at my lips, then back up at my eyes.

"Dreams about the dessert, I mean."

"That's what I meant, too." Todd's eyes locked on my lips again, then down at the ground, then back up, and he started to turn but then stopped himself. Confused, Whidbey's leash tangled up as Todd took his free hand

and rested it on the door frame. Our lips meet, and I was suddenly reminded that his kiss is definitely better than a chocolate pecan pie cupcake.

Chapter 30

The rest of spring faded as quickly as the blossoming flowers that were scattered at the base of the flagpole in the center of the condo parking lot. I had finished another round of edits to my manuscript while sitting under the ever-darkening shadows in the living room, unaware of the time. Once spotting the oven's clock I had rushed to the library before it closed because my holds were on their final day. Residents in Ocean Cove might live a slower-paced life, but it didn't show in their three-day hold library rules for books.

As I drove the short jaunt to the building, I smiled that I could once again use both hands on the steering wheel, even if clicking the turn signal caused shooting pain up my right shoulder. I felt a noticeable lessening of pain during the course of the day. The pain mostly came when I was typing, grabbing something directly in front of me, and washing my hair. Per my therapist, some motions return quicker than others, and some tasks would continue to be a challenge for a year. I had to lessen my twice-weekly physical therapy to once a week because the copays were costing me too much.

I tried to stay on top of my PT exercises at home but knew I was skipping some days because it was getting old. Somehow my phone must have figured out that I was slacking because I started getting recommendations to watch how-to-videos for all kinds of shoulder injury therapies on YouTube. There really wasn't anything you couldn't figure out how to do on your own with YouTube, be it physical therapy to counseling to installing a car engine to the precise sugar-to-water mixture for your hummingbird feeder.

"Good evening, Miss Analena. Cutting it a little close, are we?" Wendy, the librarian, said to me as she locked one side of the library doors as I crossed the threshold.

"Good evening to you, too, Wendy." I beamed a smile, making my way to the hold shelf by the circulation desk.

I pulled out the two books with my last name printed on the slip of paper, rubber-banded to the outside, and I couldn't help but think about the future of my own book. Even though I knew better, I envisioned everything playing out like all those Hallmark movies where the person manages to write a book over the weekend while she's living in her cute little cottage and sells it a week later for six figures was a fabrication. Nobody shows you the true frustration and self-doubt that follows you around every single paragraph, let alone the fact that making it would be like trying to win the lottery. Nobody tells you that you'll stare at a blank page for hours. Nobody tells you that you'll think of a great paragraph and by the time you stumble out of bed or the shower that it fizzles and reads like an owner's manual for a gas grill. Sure, in the movies the writer has writer's block, and they overcome it after going ice skating with the handsome neighbor. But that's as fake as the snow on the movie set. And it caused me to think maybe none of it was worth it. Maybe I'd wasted a year of my life?

I took the library books and squeezed them to my chest. "Ouch." I couldn't even do that without hurting my shoulder.

"Is everything alright, Nevada?"

When I turned, I spotted Mason. He was grabbing a book and DVD from the hold shelf.

"Yes, of course." I shook my head. "Mason, how are you doing?"

He was dressed in his typical button-down shirt and jeans, his gray hair in a well-kept military cut. He clutched his holds under his right arm. "My wife and I just got back from an unplanned visit to see my daughter. She was having some medical issues, and so we wanted to spend some time with her."

"I'm sorry to hear. I hope she's doing better?"

"Yes, she is. Thank you. But I'm wondering how you're doing? You look frazzled. And I don't feel that anyone in a library should ever look frazzled."

I gave a little laugh. "Yes, I agree with you."

"Anything I can do to help?"

"I would actually give anything for this to be something that help would fix, but unfortunately it's just going to take more time and effort."

"Well, you know, something that I learned from my daughter over these last few weeks was that sometimes we don't think we can do things that we can simply because we've allowed self-doubt to take over. And sometimes all we need is a reminder from somebody other than ourselves that we can do the hard things."

"I definitely feel the needle on my positivity meter is stuck on the left side of the gauge. And I'm not sure how to go about getting it moving in the correct direction."

"Does it have to do with the fact that you're writing a novel with a less-than-functional shoulder?"

"I believe that's possible." We shared a laugh.

"You know, as a child I had this grand dream to be a famous baseball player. I collected baseball cards, and I never missed the baseball games that were on TV. I played every chance I got at school, and on random neighborhood teams. I did all these things because that was my goal. When I got to high school, I'd prayed a scout would see me and recruit me. But when my father passed away, my life changed. I had to be the man of the house and provide for the family—for my mom, for my sisters, and unfortunately, my dream never came to fruition. But later in life, when I got married and had kids, I would go outside with my daughter and play catch with her, and it was at that moment that I realized that everything had happened for a reason. That my dreams changed as I had changed. I often find myself wondering if that goal had come true, would I have had the beautiful wife, kids, and grandkids I'm blessed with. Maybe there's a reason why this other path that we didn't recognize we needed was the one we're supposed to be on. In the end, you can have more than one dream, and you can always change your dreams."

I felt my shoulders slump as the weight of Mason's words wrapped up in my mind. But I appreciated what he was saying, so I nodded and smiled. "That's a great perspective. Thanks for sharing that with me."

"Take care. I'll see you around." He gave a quick nod and hurried off to get his items checked out.

I stood there for a few seconds and then checked out my books before heading back to the car with Wendy on my heels, jingling the library keys. I checked the time on my phone and realized dinnertime was hours ago, and that was why my stomach grumbled. The good angel on my left shoulder reminded me I had a bag of lettuce and plump tomatoes in the refrigerator back home. The evil angel on my right shoulder told me Alder Fish 'n' Chips is open until nine. I wasn't sure if it hurt hitting my turn signal because of the shoulder pain or because I was listening to the wrong angel.

Glancing down at my sorry-looking cookies, I couldn't help but think about the bakery cupcakes. Hopefully I've not made a grave mistake by trying to make something to bribe Todd with. The cookies were flat as though I forgot the flour, but I hadn't. They looked like a grease slick, and yet against all odds, they were quite crunchy. I took a deep breath and made a fist to knock on the door when it swung open. Todd stepped forward, clutching Whidbey's leash as he leaned out the front door.

I jumped back, tripping on the welcome mat. "I baked you some brownie cookies." I mumbled, gripping the small salad bowl with my left hand.

"Brownie cookies?" He snatched the bowl from me like a five-year-old best friend.

"They should be delicious, even if they look like the potato emoji."

"What's the occasion? I feel like you've been avoiding me for the last few weeks."

"Not you, Whidbey." I pointed at the beast, who was cautiously sniffing the bowl.

"Nice purse, hungry often?" Todd pointed.

I held up my purse, which looked like a piece of toast with butter melting on it. "A gift from my best friend, she couldn't resist."

"I guess as long as no one chases you down wanting to take a bite." Todd popped the rest of the brownie cookie into his mouth. "So, you weren't avoiding me?"

"I needed to focus on getting the latest rounds of edits done."

"And did you?"

"Yes. But I'm feeling rather unsure about it."

"You specialize in unsureness."

"Ha ha," I enunciated with such exaggeration I nearly rolled my eyes. "I wanted to see if you might be willing to—"

"Yes."

"But I didn't even tell you what I need."

"That's what sureness looks like." Todd took a bite of the cookie.

"Contractors."

"Writers."

We both narrowed our eyes at each other.

"Thank you for the brownie cookies." Todd set the bowl on the entrance table and readjusted the leash in his hand.

"You're welcome."

"So, about the manuscript, I was wondering if you could read it and give me your thoughts? My friend Amy wants to read it but she's too busy at the moment."

"You want me to beta read?"

"How do you know that term?"

"I'm a bookworm, a bibliophile. I'm also an ARC reader for some indie authors."

I blinked. "You are?"

"Don't act surprised."

I shook my head. "I didn't mean to. It's just . . ."

"Were you expecting me to wear steampunk spectacles while smoking a pipe in my winged-back chair?"

"No, of course not. You wouldn't look good in that style of glasses."

Todd placed his hand on his chest and mouthed, "Ouch."

"I can email you the file, if that works."

"That works. Should only take me a weekend. How many words is it?"

"About sixty thousand. It's a little on the shorter side, but I'm still within the correct word count for the genre, and I expect with more edits that it'll change." I slid my phone from my front short pocket and opened my email app.

"I look forward to reading it." Todd glanced down at my phone.

"Your email?"

"Yeah, it's . . ." He waved his left hand in a never mind. "It's . . ."

I widened my eyes.

"It's . . . Whidbey's dad at Hotmail."

I pinched my lips. "Hotmail?"

Todd didn't respond.

I held back a laugh. "Apostrophe?"

He shook his head, and I finished saving it into my contacts. "I'll send you the file in a few."

"Want to join us on our walk?"

"I actually have my PT appointment I need to get to."

Todd grabbed another brownie cookie and stepped outside with Whidbey, shoving the key awkwardly into the lock. I kept my distance and hurried down the stairs first.

"How's the shoulder doing?"

"It's still on my body."

"I heard most people like it there."

My posture straightened, and I stood taller as we reached the bottom of the landing. I've noticed that while I remained fearful of Whidbey, my pulse seemed to race a little less each time I saw him.

We made our way through the parking lot and stopped at my car as I readjusted the purse on my left shoulder.

I backed up against my car and spun around. "Can I make you dinner?" I know I shouldn't offer this; cooking is hard enough, but I couldn't help it.

"Yes, I'd like that."

I nodded and unlocked the driver's side door. I tossed my purse onto the passenger seat and stood back. Whidbey thought the open door was an invitation, and he lunged after my purse. Todd's arm went flying forward as I squealed and leaned back. Todd ended up directly in front of me, our eyes locked as our chests were nearly touching. Internally I panicked as though I'd never been this close to a man before. *Did I remember to brush my teeth?* I could smell spearmint coming off his breath as the slightest hint of light green flicked past his tongue. Gum. I smiled closemouthed, just to be safe, but his lips were right in front of mine. It felt like our stomachs were touching, but I couldn't look down, I couldn't look away, I sucked my stomach in, not because I didn't want them to touch but because I was as bloated as a marshmallow in the microwave.

"And that's what you get when your purse looks like buttered toast," Todd said as his eyes drifted into my car.

"It's not a purse. It's a crossbody handbag, and it's cute."

He walked around the front and opened the passenger side. "Come on, Whidbey, it's not time for a ride."

Whidbey jumped onto the pavement, and Todd paused, clutching the leash with both hands in front of him. "I'll see you for dinner . . ."

"Sunday?" I smiled. "Six thirty?"

"Sounds good. Oh, wait." Todd jogged back around, then stopped in front of me.

Is he going to kiss me? I pressed my lips together.

"Let me get your seat belt."

I climbed in as he pulled the seat belt from the holder and reached it toward the steering wheel. Taking it in my hand, I buckled it in. Even though I really wanted a kiss, at least he remembered how hard it was to reach the buckle myself.

"I hope you have a great PT session." Todd took a step, holding Whidbey back.

"Me too. Thanks again for helping me with everything."

"My pleasure." He shut the door and gave me a wave before heading toward the path he walks Whidbey on.

I couldn't help but watch him walk away, wondering how different life would be if I could stay here, if I became a best-selling author, if I could overcome my fear of dogs. As I started up the car, I also thought maybe everything so far, like Mason mentioned, was leading me down the exact path my life was supposed to be on.

Chapter 31

Summer

"This has been the longest weekend of my life," I said aloud to the empty condo.

Todd's truck hadn't moved to a different spot in the parking lot all weekend. And I'd not seen him coming or going since I left for my PT session or the grocery store to get the ingredients for dinner.

"Does his silence mean the manuscript is so good he can't stop reading or is it because it's so bad he can't face me in passing?" I asked aloud.

The timer on the oven went off, and I hurried to hush it up. I pulled the eight-by-eight dish out of the oven one-handed, because even though my therapist said my shoulder was healing, I still had a long way to go to regain my strength.

"Thank goodness the recipe didn't call for a nine-by-thirteen dish." I set it on top of the stove, the glass clanging on the surface.

The smell of ground beef, cheese, and taco seasoning circled the kitchen, and I breathed in deeply, moaning an exhale of delight.

After double-checking my makeup in the bathroom mirror, straightening my shirt, as it somehow hooked the top part into the side of my bra, I glanced at my fitness watch. It was doing its lovely vibrate reminder that I need to move. "I am moving. You really should have a shock feature for when I reach inside the freezer for ice cream."

I glanced down at my figure. The shoulder injury took what few pounds I managed to lose and helped me gain them back, plus five more. I wasn't feeling sexy, which was a good thing because it helped me not want to long for Todd as much.

It was two minutes to six thirty, and I glanced around the condo, making sure everything was as perfect as could be. Outside, the sun was still high in the western part of the sky. Summer light on the Washington coast was incredible to witness. It was so odd not to hate the sun like we did in Nevada, just wishing for it to set at the end of an August day. Here they welcome that it stays light until nine because it didn't come out often, and when it did, it wasn't trying to fry you like bacon.

A knock, soft but loud enough for me to hear, came from the front door.

"Hey," Todd said as I stepped aside for him to come in. Whidbey followed.

"Had to bring him along?"

"Yes. He loves people who hate him."

I smiled and swiped the bottle of Tempranillo off the counter.

"I don't hate him. I just like it when he keeps his distance."

Todd laid the blanket he had tucked under his arm on the carpet and instructed the dog to lie down on it. "Place." He gave Whidbey a pet and stood up. "Smells great."

"Yes, it's a taco casserole. I followed the directions exactly, so it should taste like four-point-eight stars."

Todd laughed. "I'm not sure how I feel about eating stars."

I lifted the foil top off the dish as steam wafted out. I took a quick picture and made a mental note to post it later on social media. After setting my cell down, I picked up the bag of corn tortilla chips and set it on the peninsula. "The suspense is figuratively killing me. It's creating an ulcer in my stomach."

"About the casserole?"

I removed two plates from the cupboard. "No, your thoughts about my story."

"Let's eat first."

I glanced at him, giving him a bewildered puppy-dog face.

"What? I'm starving."

This is bad. "Right, before it gets too cold."

I handed Todd the wine opener because unless it was a screw top, I fumble for ten minutes with my shoulder on the fritz. Then I point at the chip bag, too. "Would you mind this as well?" *Yep, you need strength in your shoulder to open a bag of tortilla chips.*

The condo was so silent all I heard was Whidbey sniffing heavily as his nose continued to scan the air. I focused on serving up the casserole as I pondered why Todd wanted to wait to tell me. I remind myself, don't assume. Maybe it was such a great manuscript that he was too embarrassed to admit he couldn't figure out the twist ending. Or maybe there were an unholy number of grammar errors, but he loved the story anyway. The sound of the wine being poured into two glasses pulled me from my thoughts.

"Go have a seat. I'll get the rest." Todd handed me a glass of Tempranillo.

I eased onto the high bar chair and took a big gulp of wine.

Todd lowered my plate of taco casserole in front of me in what felt like slow motion. He pulled out the chair next to me and sat down.

He picked up his fork. "Did I ever tell you about how Whidbey failed puppy obedience class?"

I shook my head and glanced around him as the dog lay almost asleep on the blanket.

"He did well with the basic commands, loved other people and the dogs in class, no fighting or dominance issues. But when it came time for us to be separated and for him to work on stay, that's when all hell broke loose. I would drop the leash, give him the command and then take a step back, then another. His bottom would remain seated, but by the time I'd backed up ten feet, Whidbey had moved five feet forward. He just couldn't do it." Todd laughed. "The trainer would tie his leash to a tree, and by the time I was ten feet away, he had to be unclipped to prevent hurting himself. His trainer wanted me to practice at home. So, I tied him to the couch leg, and he dragged the couch across the room. I tried a gazebo post, and he buckled the wood and almost pulled the post free of the railing."

I covered my mouth, laughing at the thought. "Oh, that's so sweet. How much he loves you, but also sad. He must have been scared about you not being there."

"He was, but I worked with him every day because it was nearly impossible for me to go to work or run errands."

"He seems okay now."

"He is pretty good now, although some days he comes to work with me. Some things just take more time than others. Maybe that's a universal problem. In life, people don't allow enough time for something to become wonderful."

I slowed down my chewing, thinking about what he said. He was correct, how many times I wanted to give up, move on, assuming nothing was going to be good if I waited. "He's a great dog."

Todd turned and looked at Whidbey. "He is, and I'm glad I get to be his dad because I think if he ended up with another family who might not have worked to help him, and he would be right back in the shelter he came from. Plus, he's great with my son."

"Speaking of Dylan. I haven't seen him around lately."

"I see him less in the summer. His mom keeps him busy with activities. Since I work more this time of year, she gets him more often. I'm okay with that. She's remarried, and he really needs two sets of eyes on him."

"Whidbey's don't count?"

"I wish." Todd held up his wineglass. "I completely for-got—cheers, this meal is great."

We clanked glasses.

I picked up a chip and scooped another bite of casserole onto it. "Okay, just tell me."

Todd raised his hands in the air as though he was being held up. "Okay, okay, I get Dylan next weekend."

I fight the urge to smack his arm only because the closest one is on my injured side. "Not that, but I'm glad you get to see him soon. I mean my manuscript."

He doesn't look at me, instead he's staring at his plate. "I've always prided myself on being honest, Analena."

Oh, no, he used my name. *This is bad*. My stomach twisted in knots, and I couldn't eat another bite. I pushed my left elbow onto the peninsula.

"The writing is good. The story itself . . . is well, it's . . . I think with some rewrites it could really—"

"Oh, no." I buried my face in my hands. Tears formed as I felt Todd's hand on my back.

"I'm sorry, Analena, I didn't want to *not* say anything. I care about you, and I want to see you succeed, and I think that if you could do some rewrites, it would really shine."

"Revisions are for editing. Rewrites are for utterly horrible writing," I mumbled through my tears.

"That's not what I said."

"I appreciate the feedback, but now I've just wasted your time and a year of mine with nothing to show."

"Don't say that." Todd's hand rested on top of mine, his fingers brushing my knuckles. "Every writer has several drafts they have to work on. Some even scrap entire ones because they just don't work once they're on paper."

"But it's not a first draft. I sent you a polished manuscript. I don't have time to do revisions, or to rewrite, or something else at this point. This was my once-in-a-lifetime shot."

"Why? Are you dying?"

"No, I'm not dying. I have to go back to Nevada, to my life there, my job, the one that provides me with income and health insurance. I can't spend my days writing."

"But you don't work seven days a week. You can carve out time."

Then I'm hit with a double whammy. Not only is my manuscript terrible, but I was right that nothing could ever develop between Todd and I or else he would've mentioned wanting me to stay in Ocean Cove.

Chapter 32

"Please understand I only told you because I care." Todd held a chip to his mouth.

"No, I completely understand," I stated, taking another sip of wine. Forget the casserole, I wasn't hungry anymore. "I'm just trying to process the information."

"You're crying."

"It's the taco seasoning, it's pretty strong."

"It wasn't a problem before I told you."

"It's a layering effect." I scooted out my chair and stood. "I'm feeling sort of tired. I think I need to go lie down."

"Analena, honestly, don't take it personally."

"Don't take it personally?" I went to cross my arms, and the sharp pain reminded me that I hadn't been able to do that in two months. *I can't even angrily cross my arms.* I scrunched up my face and leaned my head back. "Todd, I take it personally because it is. It's an entire year of my life gone. Instead of ending with a great accomplishment, it's ending in disgrace, defeat, and heartbreak."

"Why?"

"Are you seriously asking that right now? You said my story sucked."

Todd raised his pointer finger in the air. "No, I never said that. I said it needs some work."

"Don't you understand? I don't have time for that. This was my only shot, and I blew it."

"It's a minor setback. All you have to do is work on it. It's not like you're starting from scratch."

"You just don't understand." The tears continued to fall as I made my way to the front door.

Whidbey sprung up, and Todd grabbed him by the collar before he could reach me. I opened the door and watched Todd and Whidbey shuffle out of it. I shut it, grabbed my wineglass, and made my way to the couch.

The decorative couch pillow was soaked when I eased up into a seated position. Outside the living room slider, the sun was up as I wiped my face with the back of my hand and checked my phone to see it was well past breakfast time. My mind went to last night. In all fairness, I don't think I overreacted. What type of writer wouldn't? If you spent a year on something, anything, and it doesn't turn out the way you wanted, of course you're going to be crushed. There was no positive spin to put on it.

My stomach grumbled as I headed into the kitchen and retrieved the blue mug Todd got me, then put it back and grabbed the fall one from the cupboard. But before I could hit the coffee maker's button, there was a soft knock at the door.

I shuffled to the door and, without looking, swung it open. "Sorry, I'm not in the mood for company."

Todd sighed. "I know, but you need to eat. And I can't eat this whole croque madame myself. I offered to share it with Whidbey, but he said he didn't find the cheese to pair well with the mimosas." He held up two bags.

I blinked.

"Joking, he doesn't talk." Todd wiggled the bags.

"Fine, come in." I grimaced, looking down at the state of myself as I stepped aside.

"I wasn't going to just sit around my place knowing you were probably hungover and hungry after how we ended things last night." Todd set the bags on the countertop.

"I'm not hungover."

He pointed at the empty Tempranillo bottle on the coffee table.

"Maybe a little." I made my way past him and caught wintergreen mixed with the scent of deep woods. *Can he smell bad just once?!* If they baked gorgeous men like they do gingerbread men, then *ding,* time's up, he's done.

Todd yanked the cork from the champagne and held it over the sink as a little bubbled out. Then he moved farther into the kitchen and opened a few cupboards until he located the plates, wineglasses, and did the same for the drawers. With everything he needed, Todd glanced my way as I leaned into the counter's lip and rested my bad arm on the counter, watching him.

"I want to say I'm sorry." Todd plated the sandwiches.

"No, I should say I'm sorry for overreacting."

"No, I *want* to say it, but I can't because *I'm* not. I'm not sorry for being honest with you. Everything in life can't be perfect, especially your first attempt. Being sorry is for when you did something wrong, and your story is far from wrong."

"But it's far from right, too."

"You're the writer, you can fix it."

"That's debatable."

Todd slid my plate over and handed me a mimosa. "No, it's not. You wrote something, and whether you do revisions or put it in a drawer, you did what you set out to do. You completed the manuscript in a year. You wrote a story and finished it. The rest is time, revisions, and publishing, which is mostly all about luck. Really, have you read some of the junk they publish these days? Some real stinkers out there. But someone, some editor, at some point, loved it."

"So, what you're saying is maybe it's you that can't appreciate my story."

Todd crossed his arms. "I appreciate your story, but I know that you can make it better. And when you take a good, honest look at it, I think you will see what I see."

"There's no point."

"Don't be like that."

"Like what? Honest, like you?" I bit into the warm sandwich, and it melted on my tongue. I washed it down with a long drink of my mimosa. "I'm moving back to Nevada in a month. My time is up. I have a life to get back to, one that pays me."

"So, you won't consider staying? I never hear you mention anything back home that brings you happiness."

"The plan was never to stay, regardless of what I have or don't have back in Nevada. This was a yearlong sabbatical allowing me to focus on my dream." I returned to my sandwich and whispered, "And I was never supposed to meet you."

"I never thought I'd meet someone like you." Todd looked at my lips and then back at my eyes. "Life doesn't go as planned, even if you have a plan."

"But if you had finished reading the manuscript and said it was brilliant, then maybe my life wouldn't have had to go back to the way it was."

"It doesn't have to be. It's your life to make."

"Maybe I can at some point very far down the road."

Todd grasped my hand, and I lost myself in his eyes as he leaned in and wrapped his arm around me.

I turned and tried to hug him back, but when I reached up, I moaned. "Oh, crap, my shoulder."

Todd froze as I slipped my arms out from around him and stepped back. "Are you okay?"

"Oh, it hurts."

"It's alright, you probably just overstretched it. What does the hurt feel like?"

I placed my hand on my bicep. "It's thumping like it has a heartbeat, sort of like a twitch."

"Can you still move it?"

I try. "Yes, just feels extra weak."

"You'd know if you really messed something up. It sounds like you overdid it. That's part of this whole healing process. Chutes and Ladders." Todd rubbed the side of my arm, which was helping. "You're still doing the physical therapy, right?"

"Yes, but I'm not even going once a week anymore. It's too expensive."

"Are you still doing your exercises on your own?"

I winced. "Not so much. I'm so tired of doing them. I'm frustrated because nothing seems to really be improving. So, I'm only doing them in PT. I'm not sure how I'll return to work at the grocery store if I'm not better."

"It takes time. I know they told you that, but keep at it. You'll turn the corner." Todd took my good hand and led me to the couch. "Can you take any additional time off because of the injury when you return?"

"I'm out of money."

We sat down, and our knees touched. "Remember to pause. Spelled P-A-W-S."

I looked at him, my forehead squished in question.

Todd squeezed my hand in his. "I worry about you. All worked up and wrapped up in your thoughts. You'll work yourself into a mess if you don't take a pause. P-A-W-S. Whidbey reminds me every day. And with you leaving, I can't be there to remind you."

"I'll remember." I looked at him. "Why does life have to be real and not like in the movies?"

"Right, otherwise you would own the most beautiful home, clothes, and cars all on a rather seemingly low-paying job."

"That's why we can't date. I never ran into you and spilled coffee on you."

Todd chuckled. "If I could think of a way for you to stay, do you think we could give dating a shot?"

I blushed. "Yeah, we could."

Todd let go of my hand, stood and kissed me on the forehead. He grabbed our breakfast and brought it over to the coffee table.

"Thanks." I picked up the sandwich. "Would you like to stay for a movie? We never did our celebration movie."

"I would, but I still need to walk Whidbey, and I have a job across town that I need to get to by ten."

"Okay."

"It's not because I don't want to."

"I know."

"It sort of feels like when a series is over."

I looked at Todd, unsure of what he meant.

"You know when you watch a show that has ten seasons and then it ends, and you sort of stare off into space trying to figure out what you're possibly going to watch next?"

"Ah, that I understand."

"Good, because that's how I feel about you leaving."

And all I can think about is that I would very much like to stay in Ocean Cove and see about writing a love story of my own.

Chapter 33

Revisions and rewrites could be humbling, much like the incline on the treadmill. I'd been elbow-deep in analyzing Todd's helpful but hurtful notes that he added to the comment section on the side of my manuscript. It was nice to find little messages where he praised something he read, and a few others that made me blush. Nothing beats finding a comment that said, *I like this sentence, like I like you.* Or *Beautifully written description, like your eyes.* I guess I'd finally forgiven him for his honesty, even if there was really nothing to forgive. Should honesty inherently have an apology attached to it?

After our breakfast, I'd only seen Todd a handful of times, most often with Dylan and Whidbey walking along the shore or gone as he had a few extra projects at the height of the roofing season. My shoulder was a whole fifteen percent better, and I could wash my hair with both hands, but it still took me three attempts to secure my bra. I had only a few more PT sessions before I would be discharged.

It was another beautiful mid-August day; the sun had warmed up the sand along the shore, and families with sand toys and blankets dotted the water's edge as the afternoon dragged on. My cell phone rang on the desk. Todd's name appeared on the caller ID.

"Hey, how odd of you to call. Do people of our generation still do that?" I leaned back in the patio chair and bumped my knee on the underside of the desk and muffled a groan. "Todd?"

"I need you to do me a favor. I can't get a hold of Janet. I think she's out of town."

My heartbeat reeved up. "What do you mean?"

"I need you to grab Whidbey and watch him for a bit. He's been inside all day."

I laughed and sighed with building anxiety. "You're funny. Nice try, I'm not falling for your two-pronged plan."

"Analena. I'm at the hospital."

I sucked in so much air I coughed. "What wait? Are you okay? What happened?"

"There was an incident at my job site. I need you to take care of Whidbey."

Stumbling to stand, my free hand went to my chest as the patio chair fell backwards. "What about Piepie?"

"Right, Piepie." There was a long pause. "She and Frank are at a wedding."

"Are you sure you're okay?"

"I will be, but I can't come home, and the doctor said I'll have to stay overnight for observation."

"Observation? Shouldn't I come to the hospital or call your family or something?"

"My mom and sister live in Oregon, and Whidbey is my family. Thankfully, Dylan's back with his mom for a few more weeks."

"Overnight for observation sounds bad."

"Nah, not too bad. I fell off a ladder and hit my head. I guess I have a concussion, and I have a radial fracture of my wrist."

"Todd! That's bad."

"Comes with the job. Can you please take care of Whidbey? His food is in the refrigerator, portioned out for the week and labeled, so you really just need to make sure he pees, poops, and eats."

I bit my lip, and pinched my eyes closed. "Of course. How do I get into your place?"

Todd let me know about his secret key, and I spent several minutes trying to get my shaking hand to unlock the door. My thoughts darted back and forth between worrying about Todd and worrying about Whidbey attacking me and subsequently me joining Todd in the ER.

"I can do this. It's just a dog."

I'd been around Whidbey enough to know how to clip and hold the leash and some of the commands the dog knew. And I'd read a few books that described these fluffy creatures as being able to sense people and their needs, and I needed him to know I needed him to be calm.

I eased the front door open, and Whidbey's nose instantly greeted me, poking out.

"Sit, Whidbey, sit." My voice shook.

Squeezing past the door and the frame, I shut it with force, equally fearful of the dog escaping as I was of him attacking. I spotted the leash on the hook and kept my vision on Whidbey, who sat nicely next to the entryway console table. His tail swished back and forth on the carpet, and his tan front paws did a little bouncy dance. Gosh he was massive.

My hands shook as I pulled the clip back with my thumb and leaned forward, trying to keep as much distance as possible. I slid the collar around and secured it as Whidbey's back end popped up.

"Sitttt," I dragged out the word. "I must have a lot more feelings for your dad than I thought to be doing this."

Whidbey looked up at me, his amber eyes so adoring, as I wrapped the leash around the locked front doorknob. I didn't need him following me around as I gathered up the supplies to bring to my place.

My hands were full. I had the food, his favorite stuffed toy, a few other toys, and his blanket. I could use my bowls for serving and water. I gazed over at Whidbey and then back at the pile in my hand. If I tried to carry this and hold the leash going downstairs, I might as well assume I'll destroy my left shoulder. I set the items down, then undid the leash from the doorknob and secured it to the console table.

"Now," I pointed. "You sit and I'll be right back. Don't you try to pull this table down the stairs. Stay, I'll be back. Stayyyy."

Squeezing back through the door, I hurried down to my condo, dropped off the stuff, and jogged back up the stairs. I stood in front of the door and took a deep breath, then opened it.

"Okay, now you know you scare me, so you must be on your best behavior. Like Santa Claus is watching." I untangled the leash. "In your case, Santa Paws."

I backed up towards the door, allowing as much slack as possible on the leash. "Nice and slow." We both made it outside onto the welcome mat. "Sit."

I locked the door and then we made our way down the stairs, with enough space between us for someone carrying double bags of groceries up the center of the staircase.

"Oh, right, you need to potty." I held the leash out in front of me, wiggling it as though doing so would make Whidbey move forward like a horse pulling a horse-drawn carriage.

I'd always seen Todd take him to the side of the building in the little grass area. "Come, let's go potty."

But after several minutes of Whidbey sniffing and nothing happening, I repeated, "Go potty." More sniffing. "I know you must have to go."

My shoulder was starting to ache from all the extra movement, and holding a leash was something new for me. "Come on, why are you not going?" I stared at the dog, thinking about Todd. "Ahh . . . go pee."

Whidbey then relieved himself as I laughed. "Men."

We made it back to my condo, and I was grateful when I commanded him to "place" on his blanket, and he listened. But I was still trembling as I poured myself a glass of merlot to try to calm my nerves. I stared at Whidbey, who honestly looked sad and kept sighing every time he shifted, like his accommodations were not the five-star resort he'd booked.

"Sorry, fella, but you're lucky you're at least here instead of alone in your condo."

I sipped the chilled wine and smiled. I'd overcome a lot in the last ten minutes. After a few more minutes, my nerves calmed down a bit, and the shaking stopped. Boy, did that dog know how to make me feel guilty about him not being right next to me. I checked the time on my cell. Todd had said Whidbey ate dinner at five sharp, and if I missed it, he would be sure to let me know.

"I doubt you can tell time. And I need to finish at least three more pages of rewrites before I can call it quits for the day."

Taking my wineglass to the desk, I positioned the chair so I could at least see Whidbey out of the corner of my eye if he decided to move. My shoulder was sore, but I readied myself and dove in reworking sentences and paragraphs to switch up the plot. As the time ticked by, I heard whining to my right. I turned around and spotted Whidbey sitting up on his blanket, his tail swishing back and forth when we made eye contact. The clock in the corner of the tablet showed 5:06 p.m.

"You're okay." I returned to the screen and worked some more, trying to drown out the whimpering and shifting of fur to my right.

By 5:18 I could no longer take Whidbey's racket and sighed, gently closing the tablet. "Fine, I'm done."

The second I slouched into the patio chair, something damp touched my bare arm. "Aaaaah!" I stumbled sideways, nearly bringing the chair with me as though I'd been tied to it.

"Wooooo!" I regained my balance and stood up straight. "What happened to place?"

Whidbey trotted back to his blanket and sat. I swallowed and glanced around, then thought what had I said. "Oh, crap, *done* is your release word."

Again, the dog leaped out of place, running full speed at me. I waved my left hand and shouted, "Sit!"

Whidbey's paws dug into the carpet and his nose halted a few inches from my stomach. I pointed. "Place."

The dog sauntered over and flopped down on the blanket with a whine.

"Well, you don't need to be so dramatic, I'll get you d—" Not wanting to risk it, I hurried to the refrigerator where I'd placed Whidbey's meals and removed a container.

I located a bowl with low sides and scooped the wet food into it, adding some water as Todd had instructed on the phone earlier. Bringing the bowl to my nose, I sniffed it. "Wow, I think you might have a better meal than I do. This actually smells . . . edible, no, delicious."

After setting the bowl down at the edge of the kitchen's tile flooring, I climbed onto the high bar stool at the peninsula and said, "Done."

Whidbey's back end popped up and he dove for the bowl, causing it to slide further into the kitchen. I giggled. His tail swished back and forth as he scooted the bowl with each lick until it was empty and all the way into the corner by the oven.

"That was impressive." I watched as he lapped up his water, dripping enough from his jowls to create a small lake on the floor. "Place."

Whidbey did as he was told, and I picked up the food bowl, set it in the sink, dried the pond up, and rinsed out his water bowl, filling it back with a fresh supply. I set my good arm on my hip. "I guess you'll need to use the facilities now."

I had to admit it was weird to have to take care of something other than myself. In a way, it was nice not being alone in the condo, having another breath filling the silence. Plus, Whidbey had even made me laugh a few times with cute or silly things he did. I didn't want to admit it to Todd, but I was starting to see why someone might have a dog. Not more than one of course, like Piepie's zoo.

There was a knock at the door, and Whidbey let out a bark, causing me to jump. "You stay in place." One thing was sure with taking care of the beast: I was getting good at pointing.

When I opened the front door, Piepie was standing outside. *It's like she knows when I'm thinking about her.* "Hey, what brings you by? I thought you had a wedding to attend."

Piepie waved her hand at me but didn't speak for a few seconds. "Oh, no . . . that . . . well, yeah. That starts later."

"Later than six?"

"Yeah, odd couple." She peeked around the frame of the door. "I heard you had a guest." She rubbed her hands together.

"You don't, do you?" I observed her hands, making sure she was guinea pig free, or who knows with Piepie, she might be hiding a turtle in the palm of her hands.

She laughed, throwing her head slightly backwards. "Oh, Analena, you and your animal jokes."

I scrunched up my nose. *What joke? It's a fact.*

"I had to come and see for myself as I thought pigs were flying because there is no way. Then Sheryl came by and asked if I was aware as she saw you with Whidbey. She insisted that her sunglasses were clean. You know they are always smudged like some four-year-old with a peanut butter and jelly sandwich." Piepie crossed her hands over her chest. "Have you heard again from Todd?"

"No, just the initial call. He sounded fine on the phone and said he's there for observation."

Now I was worried. Had I shrugged off Todd's injury because he made it seem like it would all work out okay. I was so consumed by thoughts of caring for Whidbey that maybe I didn't do a good enough job making sure Todd was indeed going to be alright.

Piepie's hand found my wrist. "Are you alright? You look pale."

I shook my head, clearing my disastrous thoughts. "Yes, just need to get my food going and take Whidbey for his allotted outings."

"Is your shoulder better?"

I looked down at it as though it was not attached to me. "It's getting there, as slow as humanly possible."

"Need help taking Whidbey for a walk?"

A bark came from the left of me.

"That would be nice. Maybe it will wear him out. He's been inside all day."

"Perfect. But he probably just ate so we need to walk slowly, so he doesn't get bloat." Piepie stepped inside, spotted his leash on the counter and hooked it up like a pro. "What's his release word?"

"D-O-N-E," I spelled out as I slipped my flip-flops on.

"Alrighty, Whidbey, done." Piepie snapped on the leash like a pro, and we headed for the front door.

A small part of me hoped someday I could be as cool as Piepie.

Chapter 34

I begged Piepie to spend the night after the late-night wedding as though we were elementary school best friends, but she laughed and nicely declined. Making a comment that I could easily handle a good boy like Whidbey.

"Alright, Whidbey. You'll sleep here in place, and I'll be in the bedroom. Your dad said you can make it all night without using the facilities." I stood at the doorway to the bathroom, a prepared toothbrush in my hand, my pajamas mostly on.

Whidbey turned around in a circle two times then curled up. His head wiggled a bit as he gave a final sigh. I finished brushing my teeth, turned off all the lights but the one over the stove, shut my bedroom door, and climbed into bed. My eyes adjusted to the dark as I stared at the ceiling. A soft whimper came from out in the living room. But I knew he was safe, so I flipped over to my good shoulder, fluffed the pillow a bit with my head, and closed my eyes.

With each passing minute, Whidbey's whimper grew louder and closer together. I kicked off the covers and stomped the three feet to the door, opening it. He was facing me, sitting up in place.

"You're not getting in bed with me."

Whidbey tilted his head to the left and I tapped my foot.

"Alright." I spun around, snatched the pillow off the bed and made my way to the couch. "I'll sleep here, that way you can see me, so you don't think you're all alone." I adjusted the pillow and laid down, pulling the blanket from the back of the couch over my body.

"Good night, Whidbey."

After a few seconds, I peeked out of the corner of my eye to see that he'd laid down but not curled up like last time. Now he was spread out like the Sphinx, resting his head between his front paws.

The vibration and ding from my cell phone pulled me from my sleep. Morning sunlight filtered through the edges of the closed curtains, casting thin strips of light across the walls. My hand smacked the phone, and I pulled it to me, realizing it was ringing and not a text.

"Hello?" I rubbed the sleep from my eyes.

"Analena, good morning. How's Whidbey?"

Ah, Todd. I sat up and glanced over at the blanket. It was empty. No dog. No Whidbey. *Oh my Lanta, I lost the dog!*

"Analena? Hello?"

I covered my mouth to keep from gasping my fear right into the phone. But when I swung my feet off the couch, they touched something furry. At some point during the night, Whidbey must have left his place and curled up at the side of the couch, just under my head.

"Hey, hi, hello." I held the phone away from my mouth and sighed in great relief. "Yes, all is well. Whidbey is doing great."

The dog came onto his back legs and rested his chin in my lap. I gave his head pet after pet, running my hands over his ears, elated I'd not lost him. His fur was so soft, like a fake rabbit's foot key chain from my childhood.

"Good, I'll be home in a few hours. They're getting ready to discharge me. See you both soon. Bye."

"Bye." I tapped End and looked at Whidbey as I continued to pet his furry head.

Then my eyes grew wide, and I pulled my hand back.

"What is happening?" The dog's chin was on my lap, my hand was on his head, I'm petting him. I looked at my hand. It wasn't trembling or shaking or anything. I brought my hand to my chest, feeling around for my heartbeat, and it was soft, not racing. "My temporary fears are numbing my regular fears. I thought he was lost, and so I just momentarily forgot that I'm afraid of animals. That's all."

Whidbey lifted his chin off my lap, and something in me stirred, thinking back to how sweet it was, how much comfort he brought me, even in that moment. And now his body was touching my leg, and I was okay. I wasn't afraid. I wasn't dying. It felt sort of nice. It felt like love. Was Whidbey growing on me?

"Well, shoot." I eased my hand forward, gently patting the top of Whidbey's head. "We can't let your dad know about this. He'll think he won."

Whidbey was sitting in place when I opened the front door, and Todd was standing there, his right wrist in some type of contraption.

"You're alive. I thought he would have eaten you. I mean per your predictions." Todd grinned.

"Correct, he didn't eat me." I stepped back as he walked inside. "How are you?"

The dog's tail smacked the wall like a hammer.

"Hey, I missed you too, buddy. Done!" Todd held his one arm wide as Whidbey crashed into him, his entire body wiggling with joy. "I'm better now."

"Are you going to be okay to care for him with your wrist like that?"

Todd stood. "Oh, this is nothing. I've taken care of Whidbey with a cast on my foot. Not easy, but we made it work."

"I don't mind helping out more if needed."

"I appreciate all you've done so far, especially with your fear of dogs."

"Right, yes." I took a few steps back, realizing I was rather close to Whidbey. "If you need help with cooking, cleaning . . ." *Taking off your shirt.* "Laundry." My face flushed. "Just let me know."

"Thanks." He reached his hand out. "Your shoulder, I hope you didn't have to do anything for Whidbey that hurt it."

I glanced down at his hand as it grazed my shoulder. "Nah, no, he was good. And Piepie helped me walk him last night. He listens, as long as you know the right command."

"He's a good boy. It's only been the two of us for years. I've never even boarded him, so he's particular with his schedule and commands." Todd glanced at the dog. "We should probably get home. I want to lie down for a bit."

"Yes, of course. Why don't I get his blanket and toys?" I gathered up all of Whidbey's items I'd brought over less than twenty-four hours ago, along with the key off the peninsula.

"Thanks." Todd and Whidbey headed out the front door. "You know, if I didn't know better, I'd say you seem a lot more at ease around him."

I followed behind them up the stairs. "Really? That might be the concussion talking."

He glanced back over his shoulder when he reached the landing and smiled.

I pointed at his wrist. "This couldn't have been part of your two-pronged plan?"

"Sometimes accidents end up working in your favor. And sometimes plans have to pivot, you should understand that."

He was right, I understood that more than I ever thought possible.

Chapter 35

Several days later, when I walked through the door into physical therapy, I spotted the most adorable dog I'd ever seen. *Sorry Whidbey. Wait, was I really starting to like . . . dogs?*

The whiteish-yellow dog was stout and tank-like. He looked nothing like Whidbey's pointed ears and intense body posture. I thought for sure if a tornado happened upon this small town of Crooked River, this dog would be the only thing left standing. I couldn't help but stare at him. He wasn't even on a leash, which for a second made me freeze, then I realized he probably has zero speed. He looked like he'd only be able to lumber along, so he couldn't chase after me. While I'd gotten better with Whidbey, even giving him a few pets when I saw him, we were far from snuggle buddies. And I still couldn't handle Piepie's guinea pigs. They were too much like plump rats ready to chat about their drama.

The dog was right next to a woman who was lifting small weights or was trying to, anyway. They must be one or two pounds, and the dog with floppy ears seemed to be smiling up at her with each bicep curl she made. As one of the trainers took the weights from her, a man in a wheelchair wheeled by.

I handed my exercise sheet to a technician. "Analena, how is your shoulder today?" she asked, not smiling but not frowning either.

"It's a shoulder."

The tech laughed. For the life of me, I couldn't remember her name, but she was usually pretty nice and kept an eye on me to make sure everything I needed was set up before I moved to the next exercise. I always started with the arm-pulley, which was the reason I wore a long shirt after my first session, because with each arm raise, my shirt turned into a '90s midriff style. When I finished that, I did some band work followed by my therapist checking in on me. Today he was across the building while I was halfway through my exercises. We usually chatted about how I'd been feeling and my range of motion since my last visit before we would joke around about food or some other current event as I worked my way through my other exercises.

"Analena, how is the shoulder feeling today?" my therapist, Chris, asked.

"The movement seems a bit better." I grinned. "What's the story with the dog?"

Chris turned to look over his shoulder and then back to me. "I'm glad you asked. Let me introduce you. They usually aren't here on the day you come in."

"I'm okay." I waved him off.

"That's like turning down a chance to meet Jensen Ackles."

"I'm okay with that."

"I'm going to pretend I didn't hear that. Come on."

"What can I say? My heart belongs to Jason Statham." I finished my final set of lateral pulls and reluctantly followed him over to the man in the wheelchair and the yellow tank of a dog.

"Analena, I'd like you to meet the famous Bayou," he pointed at the Labrador with a service dog vest on, "and Ox."

I reached my hand down to Ox, who was in the wheelchair. "Nice to meet you."

He beamed a smile. "Same."

"Your dog is adorable." I stepped back, not wanting to get too close to Bayou.

"You can go ahead and pet him." Ox glanced over at Bayou as he sat back, his bottom feet sprawling forward in a V shape around his front legs.

"Well," I muffled a laugh, "he certainly looks relaxed." I eased forward and reached my hand out with the uneasiness of a child at a petting zoo for the first time.

His fur was buttery soft, just like the color. "He's a —?"

"English Labrador."

"Oh, sorry, I don't know much about dogs. A Lab?"

"English Lab," Ox chuckled. "Don't get my wife, Kate, started on the differences between American Labs and English. She says they are the superior of the breed. Although we recently expanded our family and adopted a senior Doberman. She's been on the fence a lot lately."

"I'm on the other side of all fences. I'm not really a pet person." I stopped petting Bayou.

"Sure seems like that might be changing," Ox smirked.

I tilted my head; my mouth drew into a straight line. "So, what is it that Bayou does?"

"He helps people with anxiety. Coming here to do therapy can feel very overwhelming and at times defeating, especially at the beginning. He gives a lot of clients extra motivation to show up. And if they start to panic or feel uneasy about an exercise, he helps them by providing comfort."

"And I thought I was the only one dreading physical therapy."

"Recovering from injuries can involve a wave of emotions, from frustration to pain. I have MS, so I can understand where people are coming from, and it's the reason I got Bayou into this field. It's good for us both."

I instantly felt horrible about my inner thoughts. Here I was with some silly shoulder thing. "I'm sorry I didn't—"

Bayou stepped forward and licked my hand.

"It's okay. I don't have an MS flag waving off the back of my wheelchair; it tends to attract pigeons." He laughed, and Chris and I joined in.

I looked down at Bayou as I ran my hand over his head. I guess I'd been petting him since he licked my hand but was only now aware.

"I heard this is your last session?" Ox wheeled his chair forward as I headed to the wall for some wall stretches.

"Yes, I'm sort of concerned because I won't have the guidance and trained eyes on me doing it all by myself."

"I hate to break it to you, but you've been doing all the work this entire time."

Bayou lays down at the side of my feet as I began my first set of twenty wall-walks. "I've only been doing what they tell me."

"But Chris isn't really doing anything. He and the team give you exercises, and then you do them. You have all the power within you to heal yourself, so don't let the professionals make you think you need them. They gave you guidance; now it's up to you to follow through. It's like that with anything in life."

"I'm not sure how well I do with follow-through. My biggest plan failed."

"How so?" Ox crossed his arms, and I noticed a small tremor in them.

"I had this big dream, and it didn't pan out the way I wanted."

Ox pointed at his wheelchair. "Do you think I don't understand about dreams not coming true?"

My stomach turned with anxiety after my insensitive comment. Bayou lifted his head and pawed at my shoe a few times, so I reached down to pet his head and felt my anxiety instantly draining away.

"Just because a dream doesn't come true doesn't mean you've failed. In fact, you might have failed because it wasn't the course you were supposed to be on. Dreams are great, but reality can be greater. Maybe your goal didn't turn out the way you wanted, but maybe that was the point. I became a pilot and really wanted to expand my business, but I also ran an inn. When MS became more than a disease but my new lifestyle, I felt I had failed because I could no longer live out my dreams. Yet, from that failed dream came the expansion of Bayou's therapy dog services. It started off as more of a hobby, little jobs here and there, and now we're employed by the local dentist office and several therapy outfits, including this one. My other English Lab, River, he's in training to become one, too, as long as I can get him to stop focusing on fetch." Ox laughed. "While I miss being a pilot and our inn business finally closed its doors, the shift didn't mean new opportunities weren't around the corner. But it was a struggle to see at first."

"I think they call those happy little mistakes."

"Indeed." He folded his hands in his lap; the tremor remaining.

Bayou got up and rested his chin on Ox's lap. "I know you need to move on to your next exercise. It was great meeting you. Keep in mind, everything you need is right in front of you, because where else are you living, in the past or the future? Embrace being in love with now."

Chapter 36

Tomorrow I was leaving and heading home to Nevada, and the thought alone sucked the wind from me. I'd spent the day packing up my belongings and cleaning everything from the toilet to the stove. My arm and shoulder ached from the work, and I wished I felt happier, but the sadness of leaving spreading through me reminded me otherwise.

I took my glass of chardonnay to the balcony, the patio chair back where it belonged. Todd and Mason came over the other day, and they moved my desk to Todd's place. He insisted on shipping it to Nevada for me.

The breeze off the ocean caused me to shiver. It was the first week of September, and summer had slipped fast out of Ocean Cove as though in a hurry. I would miss so many things about this place. It really did feel like my home and a town I wanted to stay in. While the view was amazing, it was more than the abundance of water, it was life in general. Even taking out the fact that I didn't have to deal with the stresses of work, Ocean Cove felt different. I could feel it in my soul as though I was a part of everything going on around me. The vibe of life and living was different. Not to say that back home in Henderson wasn't good, it just didn't feel like me anymore and hadn't for a long time.

"Analena! Analena!" A female voice called out from the distance.

I stood and leaned over the railing to see Piepie jogging in my direction as I waved back.

"I darn near thought I'd miss you." Piepie rested both hands on her knees as she bent over.

"You didn't have to run. It's not like I was on the caboose of a train pulling out of the station."

She glanced up at me, huffing. "I can see why you and Todd make a good couple."

I shook my head. "We're not a couple. So, what are you doing out running?"

"My doctor said I need to get more exercise. I guess chasing my pets around the condo all day doesn't cut it anymore. Aging sucks."

"I hear you." I began to glance down at my body but stopped. I was trying to be nicer to myself.

"Are you sure you can't stay? You're so much more fun than the doctor Cathy. She's always walking around inspecting this or that. And she's not really the type to hang out during a beach campfire or anything."

"I wish I could stay, but . . ."

Piepie crossed her arms and smiled. "Hesitation. I like it."

"It would be far too risky to start over. I think there comes a time in life when you accept what you have and make it work. There is nothing wrong with my life back home, but it'll be hard to slip back into it after creating something different here."

"I think what you did was brave, coming here for a year, working on a dream. It might seem easy from the outside, but whatever the outcome, you did well." She squeezed my wrist. "Speaking of, did you finish the book? Did you land a book deal?"

My heart sank. I desperately wanted to tell Piepie a stream of great news, but that wasn't my luck. "I finished the book, but I'm still working on rewrites, and I don't know if or when it will be ready for the next step."

"I can tell by the sadness in your eyes you're disappointed, but don't be. You did your best. That's all you or anyone can do."

"I'm starting to see that, but it didn't—"

"The outcome doesn't matter, Analena. You spent a year living your dream."

I nodded. "You're right."

"Give me a hug. We must find ways to stay in touch." Piepie leaned over my railing as we embraced. "My book club meets virtually every month on the first Friday. We have such fun, and we have nine members. One of them is in England. You should hear her accent."

"Sounds like fun."

Her watch vibrated on her wrist. "Shoot, I've got to get to the shelter. I'm fostering two of the cutest guinea pigs until they can find someone to adopt them."

"Two? Don't you already have two?"

"Yes, but the best things in life come in twos. Frank and me." She started to jog away, spun around and called out, "You and Todd!"

I laughed and waved before returning to the patio chair with my wineglass. The sun dipped lower, causing bubble gum pink and apricot to highlight the sky over the water. Piepie was right, and the more I thought about what she said, the more guilt I felt for having a negative attitude about this year not going as expected. A part of me wanted to go back and do it all over again—not so that I could get it better or right, but so that I could live in the moment, more than I had. Why was that the way I always seemed to live my life? Not realizing what was right in front of me, focusing on the future more than the present, just like Ox had alluded to. When would I learn?

"Hey, neighbor."

I turned around in the patio chair to find Janet and Yo-Yo exiting onto their veranda.

"Good evening." I raised my glass when I spotted she had a glass of red wine in her hand.

"Tonight, is your last night?"

I nodded and held in a sigh. "Yeah."

"You've been a good neighbor. But I'm sure you're ready to get back to your life in Nevada."

I paused for a second too long and caught Janet giving me a knowing eyebrow raise. "Yes, of course, it will be good to get back into the swing of things." I buried my lips behind a long sip of chardonnay.

"No future with Todd?"

I choked, my palm smacking my chest, until I was okay. "We're friends, so I guess in a way, yes there is a future with Todd."

"If that's what you kids want to call it," Janet mumbled loud enough for me to hear her.

I spun toward the view. "I'll surely miss this."

"I don't know how you do it down there with no seasons, just desert and sun."

"We eat a lot of ice cream."

Janet laughed and picked up Yo-Yo, nestling the dog to her chest. "I heard you're doing better with dogs."

"I'm not adopting from a shelter anytime soon, but my heart doesn't try to jump out of my chest when they come near me. And I can even pet them."

"That's great! What an accomplishment."

Funny, I never really saw it that way. "Thanks."

"Say bye to Analena." Janet held up the dog's front right paw, making it wave.

I waved back. "Bye, Yo-Yo. Bye, Janet."

She headed back inside as I returned to the chair, watching as the top crest of the sun disappeared below the waterline. As the colors muted and faded from light blue to violet and finally into sapphire, the chill in the air grew. In only leggings and a T-shirt, I began to shiver. It was when I stood up, empty wineglass in hand, that I spotted the figures of a man and a dog coming down the beach. A part of me wanted to run inside, because I knew who it was, and I was not ready to say goodbye. I didn't know how to. It hurt my heart thinking about it. So of course, I hurried inside, softly closing the slider.

You're being ridiculous.

My fingers found the handle and eased the slider back open, and I stepped out. However, something in my heart warned me, and I spun around to head back inside, but I misjudged the space I needed. The wineglass smacked into the frame of the slider as I attempted to go inside. Glass shattered all around my bare feet.

"Shh-ooot!" I halted.

If I moved my feet an inch, the patio would turn into a red abstract art piece.

"I guess since it's your last night I might as well rescue you," Todd's voice appeared over the railing.

I glanced up, fearing that if I took my eyes off the glass shards, I'd wobble, and my feet would get cut. "I would actually appreciate it very much."

"Whidbey, did you hear that? She's admitting her defeat, and at such a young age."

"Hey, we're only nine months apart."

"Yes, but I'm the one who's nine months older."

My right leg was starting to cramp because I was mid-step when it happened. "Could you please hurry up your helping?"

"Right, hold on." Todd and Whidbey jogged off.

What felt like half an hour later, my doorknob jiggled. "Crap. It's locked!" I shouted.

Todd appeared moments later, climbing over the railing of my veranda with ease. I was not sure what the plan was, but my leg was shaking from the isometric hold I'd endured for the last several minutes.

He leaned forward, wrapped me in his arms, and lifted me up and over the glass, setting me down on the carpet inside. To be fair, even though he was tall and looked very strong, I knew how much I weighed, and I tried to hide how impressed I was that he lifted me as though I weighed no more than a throw pillow. Those weren't vanity muscles under his shirt.

"Hey, where is your wrist thing?"

He held up the wrist. "All better."

I glanced at my shoulder. "I wish I had that ability with my shoulder."

"I know yours is getting better. Where is your broom?"

"In the pantry." I pointed at it as though he had no idea what a pantry looked like.

After Todd had cleaned up the broken glass with the broom, he vacuumed the area. "You really didn't have to do all that." I stood up as he was putting away the vacuum. "It was my mess to clean up."

"I couldn't have you cutting your pretty toes on glass." Todd shut the pantry door. "So . . . tomorrow." He glanced around at the undecorated living room, as my few touches had been packed away into one small box that sat by the front door.

"Tomorrow." I headed into the kitchen and pulled down a new wineglass. "Thank you for the edit notes. I got through all of them."

"I'm sure your revisions will turn out great."

"Not sure; I still have a long way to go." I poured chardonnay into the glass and wiggled the bottle at Todd.

"Thanks, but I should get back to Whidbey, sort of left him in a rush. Don't want him freaking out."

I nodded. "Right, of course."

Todd rested his hand on the front doorknob and looked back at me. "This year has really gone by too fast."

"It has." I brought the wineglass to my lips to try to refocus my emotions that were bubbling up in the back of my throat.

"Have a nice evening." He swung open the door and stepped outside. "Night."

"Good night." I went to the door and locked it as though in slow motion.

The world around me felt so very silent, like when it snowed during Christmas, a memory I will forever hold in the forefront of my mind. The journey was over for me, but in a way, it felt like it was starting tomorrow. And I wasn't looking forward to it, as I already knew exactly what to expect.

Chapter 37

My car was packed, which was not as easy as it had been when I'd done it in Nevada, since I had the use of both shoulders.

"All ready to go?" Todd and Whidbey appeared to my right as I clumsily closed the trunk with my good arm.

"Yes, I was going to swing by and say my goodbyes to you and Whidbey." I half smiled. To be fair, I really had no idea what I was going to do. I'd shoved my emotions so deep inside of me the last few days, they were filled to the brim, and if I so much as stumbled over a sidewalk crack, they would come spilling out.

"Are you sure your shoulder can handle the long drive?" Todd switched hands with the leash as Whidbey's tail wagged with delight.

I leaned forward and gave Whidbey a long pat on his head. "I'll take it easy heading through Reno. I planned for a few overnights just to make sure I get enough breaks. I'm in no rush to get back home." *Did I just say that?* "I mean, I'm happy to get back to my townhome, with all my knickknacks, and get back into a routine." My right eye twitched at the lie.

"So, your shoulder is better, then?"

"Kind of. I think I hit that hurdle you mentioned. The one I thought would never come. But to be fair, I think maybe some magic just rubbed off on me in the form of Bayou fur."

"For *someone* who insists she's still not a pet person, *someone* mentions a therapy dog an awful lot."

"Change can be goodish."

I caught Todd's hand coming towards mine, and I allowed it, because I didn't have the strength to pull back in our final minutes together. "Oh yeah? Any other changes you're thinking of?"

"Not yet. Still percolating like a coffee pot." I smiled softly.

"Just don't let it distract you from driving."

He knew me well. My head was always filled with thoughts, causing me to lose my focus. I wasn't the type of person who should listen to podcasts or audiobooks while driving.

We stood there, holding hands just at the fingertips, knowing we wanted more, but it wasn't in the cards.

"Feels weird to be leaving. I thought I would be more at ease and eager to get back home. Tell Dylan I said goodbye. I don't know how much he'll understand."

"I will."

Todd moved from our fingertips and held my hand in his. The scent of mint and nature coming off him meant that I would never be able to smell that and not think of him. I wanted to kiss him, and I wanted him to kiss me. My heart began to melt a little on the unromantic parking lot.

"I should probably get going before it gets any later. I'm worried about hitting traffic in Portland."

"It shouldn't be too bad by the time you get there." He didn't let go of my hand; instead, he squeezed it. "I'm going to miss you."

"I'm going to miss you, too. I enjoyed my time here, the people, the community. I'm sad to go, but I have to."

"I suppose. Everything good must come to an end."

"Just like good TV series."

We stood there, staring at each other. The seagulls flew overhead, the distant sound of the waves on the beach behind us. Whidbey, at Todd's side, leaned into his leg.

Todd glanced at my lips and then back to my eyes. "It probably wouldn't be good if I kissed you, would it?"

I blushed. "Um, not really. I mean, we probably shouldn't—"

His lips found mine in record time, and he wrapped me up while my good arm found his back, but my other arm rested low on his hip. I was going to miss this the most, the way my whole body tingled when he kissed me. And somehow it was more than just a kiss, the way he held me with such care and support. I feared I would compare every other guy in my future to Todd.

Knowing this, caused me to pull back. "I really should go."

"Text me when you get there. I mean or call, let me know you arrived safely."

"Every night?"

"I care very much about you, Analena."

"I feel the same about you, but—"

"Our timing is not right. I get it—different place, different time."

"I think our timing is right. We both got the bad marriages out of the way, but the distance it just too . . ."

"Distant."

I guffawed. "Yeah."

"Drive safe, Analena."

"I will." I went on my tippy-toes, and he leaned down so I could kiss him on the cheek, then gave a final pet to Whidbey, my hand sliding from his soft fur. I climbed into the car while he helped with my seat belt because it was still painful to reach that way.

"Bye, possible burglar Analena."

"Bye, suspicious Todd."

He shut the door and stepped back with Whidbey as I started the car. Making my way out of the parking lot, I couldn't bear to turn around or look at him in my mirrors; it would only make the tears falling come faster.

Chapter 38

A week after I returned to Henderson, there was an unexpected knock at my door.

"Hey, Piepie, hold on a second." I crawled off the couch and set my cell phone on the desk Todd had built and made my way to the front door.

I opened the door and found the postal carrier standing there.

"Hi, sorry, there was no room to leave this at the mailbox." He handed me a small priority box.

"Thanks," I said and shut the door behind me, picking the phone back up, putting it on speaker.

"What was that?" Piepie asked.

"I'm not sure. I didn't order anything." I checked the return label. "Oh, it's from Todd."

"Open it!"

I returned to the couch and laughed. I opened the box and slid the item out. It was wrapped in white tissue paper.

"Well?" Piepie said. I could hear one of her dogs barking in the background.

"Hold on, I think he got me a book."

But when I got the tissue off it, I recognized the title, and the name of the author.

"It's me."

"What's you?"

"The book."

"What?"

"Hold on, there's a note." I unfold the sheet of spiral notebook paper and read it aloud.

ANALENA,

I WANTED YOU TO KNOW THAT YOU SHOULD NEVER GIVE UP. I BELIEVE IN YOU, AND YOU SHOULD TOO. THIS GIFT IS TO REMIND YOU OF THAT. SOMEDAY, THIS BOOK WILL BE AS IT IS IN YOUR HANDS. A REALITY.

HAVE HOPE,

TODD

"That is a sweet note. But what did he get you?"

"It's a mock-up book. He put '*New York Times* Bestseller' above my name on the cover. It looks like the real deal, Piepie." I flipped it over and on the back cover was the photo he took with the flash the first time I sat at my desk he made me. "Oh gosh, and he included a back-cover author photo. Here, let me send you a picture."

I snapped a picture of the front and back with my cell and hit Send.

"How cool. Analena, that's amazing. It does look real. That's the best manifestation."

"Manifestation of what?"

"Your dreams, silly. Like a vision board, only better. He's created a way for you to literally see your end goal, to help you realize it and make it happen."

I found the gift to be both wonderful and heartbreaking at the same time.

"Analena?" Piepie asked.

"It's just, I'm grateful he did this. It's so kind and thoughtful, but it's also a reminder that I miss him, and that I've got a long way to go until this author dream comes true."

"I'm sorry you miss him; he has been pretty mopey walking around. As for the book, like you said, you have something you can work with, and as soon as you knock out all those revisions, it'll happen. We know life is not like the movies.'"

I frowned. "True. I do feel like my novel year experience was really about me finding out who I've become later in life; finding out what I need to make me happy and what my priorities should be."

"Nothing wrong with that. Oh, I have to go! The guinea pigs are popcorning and I promised I'd record it so the shelter could use it as a fun adopt-me video."

"Bye, Piepie."

"Bye."

After watching three YouTube videos on what a popcorning guinea pig was, I scrolled through my contacts and texted Todd, but he didn't respond. He's probably busy standing on a roof in the rain or something dangerous. I brought the book to my nose and breathed in, but it wasn't the delightful scent of paper, it was wintergreen. It was Todd. The darn wonderfully thoughtful book smelled like Todd. A tear rolled down my cheek.

I pondered, looking around my living room. My return home had been uneventful. Amy was away on vacation with her family, and Dawson had finally moved on with his life. I'd heard that he was dating, and while I was happy for him, I still needed to get my crockpot back. But I figured that reaching out to him for any reason might result in a setback I wasn't willing to risk. Once I got going again with a regular paycheck from work, I was going to order a new crockpot. With the holidays fast approaching, there should be some good deals.

I wrapped the heating pad around my shoulder and hit three on the controller. After wiping the tears from my cheeks, I glanced out the window over the back of the couch. The palm trees danced in the wind that was picking up. I closed my eyes and brought up the view of the ocean that I had ingrained in my memory. I could feel the patio chair under my bottom, the gentle salty breeze on my face, and the moisture in my hair. I thought about Janet and Mason, Piepie, and Todd and Whidbey. I always tried to push the Todd memories to the back, they hurt the most. I pictured my fingers on Whidbey's soft black-and-tan fur.

I opened my eyes and looked around my townhome with all my things surrounding me. I no longer felt I was in the right place. I'd become a visitor here who wanted nothing more than to go back home.

Chapter 39

I'd been back at work for a week now, but only doing half shifts due to my lingering shoulder injury. I was limited to what I could lift and drag over the scanner, so I often found myself rushing to tell customers to leave the big items in the cart and I'd use the scanner wand. To which many were very happy about not having to move them an extra time.

"Analena, so good to see you again. It's been a while," Margo, a regular customer, said as she began unloading a cluster of bananas and apples onto the belt.

While she was a nice customer, polite and kind, her groceries mostly consisted of fruits and vegetables, so it was a lot of code entering because those barcode stickers were the most challenging on rounded surfaces to scan. I'd seen too many veggies lose their lives at the hands of the self-checkout at other stores.

"It has been a whole year." I scanned her bag of organic spaghetti noodles.

"How did it go?"

"It was different than I expected, but a lot of good came out of it." I smiled.

"That's life for you, right?" Margo set a bag of lettuce on the belt.

"A roller coaster, that it is."

I finished ringing up Margo and checked the time on my fitness watch as she pushed her cart towards the exit. A customer moved forward in my line, but I didn't see any groceries on the belt. He probably needed ice or stamps. I glanced up at him.

"Todd?"

He smiled and rested his hands on the payment counter. "I have a new two-pronged plan."

I laughed and held back the emotions that were about to come pouring from my eyes. "I can imagine you do. Where is Whidbey?"

Todd turned to the person behind him in line. "This is what happens when you get them to like your dog more than you. That's all they care about."

The customer grinned and nodded his head.

It took a few seconds for me to get my feet moving, and when they did, I bolted around the checkstand, and he wrapped me up in his arms. I didn't care that my shoulder was hurting as I held on tight as though we were on the bow of a ship in rough waters. I leaned back and grinned, kissing him as though we'd been apart for years. Then I heard the clearing of a throat and eased out of Todd's embrace to see my manager with her arms crossed, standing in the bagging area.

"Sorry, Todd, this is my boss, Megan, and I'm at work. Somehow, I forgot that." I straightened my apron and name tag.

"Would you like to take your lunch break now?" Megan asked.

"Yes, please."

Megan stepped into my register, and I hurried outside, pulling Todd behind me with my good arm.

The sun was blinding and warm, even with it being the end of September. We sat on a nearby bench, under a canopy, next to the store's cart return.

"What are you doing here?" I asked, still holding his hand as he set a small paper bag behind him on the bench.

"I missed you so much and didn't feel it was right to tell you how I felt over the phone."

"How do you feel?" I swallowed hard.

"I can't move. I have Dylan. I have to remain in Washington or I'll only get to see him once or twice a year, and traveling would be really challenging for him."

"I would never ask you to do that."

Todd nodded. "And I can't ask you to uproot your life here to move to Ocean Cove. But I really want to see about giving us a shot. I want us to date, go on real dates, be a real couple, see how things unfold."

"And we can't do that states apart."

"And it's too soon to buy a house and move in together; it's not a heartwarming romance movie."

"Oh, of course, we need to date for at least a year—proper dates, like you said, not just being friendly neighbors."

"You're really making me regret not asking you out as soon as I saw you move into the condo." He smiled.

"Me too, but I was there for a purpose, and a relationship was not on my list."

Todd glanced down at our hands, mine still wrapped around his. "So, what do we do?"

The woman I was a year ago would never have even so much as thought about throwing all my eggs into one basket. Thank goodness the woman I was today was different, not better or worse, not smarter . . . just different. "I've been looking into a possible career change."

"You have?"

"I have. In fact, I've spoken with Meredith over at Sealed Storage."

Todd's eyes narrowed and his brow scrunched up. "Do you have Sealed Storage chains here or are you talking about the ones in Washington?"

"I'm talking specifically about the one in Crooked River."

"Twenty-minutes away from Ocean Cove, that Crooked River?"

I nodded my head and grinned, tracing my finger over the knuckles on his right hand. "Meredith had put a job posting up looking for someone to manage the storage facility, and since it's a twenty-four-hour facility, she needed someone who could live on-site. She has part-time workers, but none of them wanted the spot."

"So, you're going to manage a Sealed Storage?"

"I'm going to live in the apartment on-site. I was drinking the night I called about the job posting. I think the alcohol had gone to my head, and I let it slip I was an aspiring author. Meredith thought it would be a great match because I could work on my story on the clock since it's a lot of sitting around."

"And she thought that even with you drunk on the phone?"

"I wasn't drunk. I was emotionally influenced. What can I say? I missed you and Ocean Cove."

"We miss you, too, even Whidbey." Todd squeezed my hand. "And when were you planning to tell me?"

"I was getting there—it just happened, with the job offer. But I want you to know I'm doing this for me. I'm moving back there for myself and the opportunity it'll bring me. Being able to devote the majority of my days to writing, editing, and getting a steady paycheck. Plus, a place to live."

"And where do I fit into all of this?"

"You're the perk."

"The perk?"

"If I moved back only because of us, then that would put too much pressure on a new relationship. I'm still feeling myself out, what I want in life, navigating through the waters, and while I want you to be on the boat with me, I don't want you to be the only one paddling."

"But I really like paddling." He flexed his bicep.

Oh gosh, I can't wait to date this man! "I think if I'd reached my goal successfully, that maybe I wouldn't have learned what I did about myself. Smooth sailing doesn't allow for discovery."

"And what wonderful things did you discover?"

"Remember when I told you what Ox said about being in love with now. I was so focused on the future and the past that I wasn't in love with now. I felt regret for what I'd not accomplished in my life and put so much weight on the writing dream that I lost sight of living and loving what I have right now. It doesn't mean I'm not disappointed in the whole book thing. But it helped me to see that just because I have plans doesn't mean they'll work out, and just because I don't have plans doesn't mean that life wouldn't work out in unexpected, pleasant ways."

"Like me, of course." Todd grins.

I leaned into him. "Yes, exactly."

We sat in silence, watching the world go by in the parking lot—people living their lives, some in a hurry, some taking their time. And I couldn't wait to do more of it with Todd.

"How long are you staying in Henderson?"

"I have a flight out tomorrow morning. I left Whidbey with Dylan's mom, figuring it would be the most familiar to at least have Dylan around. This is the longest I've ever been away from him." He wrapped his arms around me, and even though it was hot out, I nestled into him.

"Wait, what was your two-pronged plan if you were only staying twenty-four hours?"

"I was going to woo you with a puppy."

I laughed. "Why would you ever think that would work? I only tolerate pets now."

"Because no one can resist a puppy."

I pointed at my chest. "I can."

"I guess we'll see." He set the paper bag on my lap. "Here, open this."

I peered inside the bag, which contained something with white tissue paper over the top. "What is this?"

"Well, you have to open it."

I removed the top of the tissue paper and then dug around, pulling out a coffee mug. It was yellow and cream with something printed in purple. I held it up and read it: Best Mom EvFur. I gave Todd a questioning look. "It's like yours, but what does it mean? I'm not a mom."

"The shelter that Piepie works at had a litter of puppies come in, and they're looking for new homes in a few weeks once they're ready. And I thought maybe you'd want to be a dog mom."

"That's a little presumptuous."

"Maybe for a short person such as yourself, but I figured with you and Whidbey being the same height, you'd agree."

I leaned back. "Are you claiming I'm as tall as your dog?"

"Of course not, you're at least two inches taller."

I gasped, and Todd busted up laughing. "Okay, okay, Whidbey is ready for a sibling. You don't have to get a puppy. I will, but just in case you wanted to be a dog mom."

"What type of dog?"

"A Lab."

"An American Lab?" I frowned.

"Yeah, why?"

"English Labs are far superior, just ask Bayou."

"Yep, this second two-pronged plan will be easier than the first one."

"You and your plans. Have you not learned that plans have a mind of their own?" I glanced up at him, my head on his chest.

Todd shook his head. "Not when you prong them."

THE END

Author's Note

Dear Reader,

While I was working on the first draft of this novel, I injured my shoulder during a yoga move resulting in a SLAP tear. After over a month of trying to get answers as to what happened through an MRI scan and X-rays, I ended up with frozen shoulder as well. I decided to go without any medication or injections (against my doctor's advice on multiple occasions) and focused on physical therapy. I had a wonderful therapist and I truly believe that working with him specifically made all the difference in my recovery, although a slow one, he knew more than my doctor.

However, my shoulder's healing process was painful and emotional. Like Analena, I couldn't do basic things like wash dishes, type (for both writing and my day job) wash my hair, or use the turn signal in the car without severe pain. Sadly, no wonderful English Labs showed up at my physically therapy sessions. It was and continues to be a long process of healing. At the time of writing this, I'm at the year mark for the injuries and still not one hundred percent back to normal—which is typical and will continue to be something I deal with as a possible recurring issue. Thank goodness I still remember all my physical therapy exercises!

What I've learned from my injuries is the importance of focusing on what you can do and never stop overcoming obstacles in your path. It's not easy, but it does make for a stronger person in the end. And . . . it helps to add details to your . . . novel year.

Savannah

Acknowledgements

For Charley, Bayou, Ransom, and MacGyver. It was mind-bending to write a character that didn't like animals, especially dogs. I know you'll forgive me for this decision because in your short lives you managed to change many minds, much like Analena.

My PAWS Readers – Carol, Linda, Elaine, Carrie, Piepie (thanks for all your guinea pig pictures and for sharing the name story), April, Sam, Gloria, Lissa, Marabeth, Lisa, Robin, Rachel, JoAnna, Janeal, Shelle, and JoDena. Thank you for always cheering me and my stories onward.

To my auto-buy readers, it means the world to me that you honor my stories so much. And thank you for your awesome reviews.

If this is the first book of mine you've read of mine, thank you for taking a chance. If you're a returning reader, I so appreciate your decision to come back for a new read.

For D.S. – Thank you for being my first reader, my love, my life, and the best man in the world.

About the
Author

 Savannah Hendricks (born in California, raised in Washington, and resides in Arizona) is a full-time social worker and fills as much of her weekends as possible with writing. She loves all things dog-related, has a passion for red wine, gardening, baking, and creating yummy recipes. You'll often find her hollering at the TV during restoration shows when they paint over red bricks.

If you'd love a digital personalized autograph or bookplate, you can request one by visiting: savannahhendricks.com
Please discover more about Savannah by interacting with her on:

Instagram: savannahhendricks_author
Facebook: AuthorSavannahHendricks

Also By Savannah

Heartfelt Coming of Age/Women's Fiction
Sun City, 85373 (Multi-Award-Winning)
The Album (Multi-Award-Winning)
I Adopted My Mom at the Bus Station (Multi-Award-Winning)

Humorously Wholesome Romance
Route to Romance
*A Hearts of Woolsey series: **A Desert Restoration, A Desert Romance, A Desert Rivalry***
The Christmas Rental
Grounded in January (Award-Winning)
Grounded in July
To Work Out or to Wed

Meaningful Picture Books

Where Does "I Love You" Go?
The Needle-less Christmas Tree & Other Tree Tales
Winston Versus the Snow (Multi-Award-Winning)
Nonnie and I (Available in English, Spanish & Bilingual)